SHADOWS OF DISASTER

OTHER BOOKS BY
CATHY BEVERIDGE

Offside (Thistledown Press, 2001)

Chaos in Halifax (Ronsdale Press, 2004)

One on One (Thistledown Press, 2005)

Stormstruck (Ronsdale Press, 2006)

Tragic Links (Ronsdale Press, 2009)

Shadows
of Disaster

Cathy Beveridge

RONSDALE PRESS

RONSDALE PRESS
3350 West 21st Avenue
Vancouver, B.C., Canada
V6S 1G7

Set in Minion: 12 pt on 16
Typesetting: Julie Cochrane
Printing: Island Blue, British Columbia
Cover Art: Ljuba Levstek
Cover Design: Julie Cochrane
Author Photo: Andrew Platten

Ronsdale Press wishes to thank the Canada Council for the Arts, the Government of Canada through the Book Publishing Industry Development Program (BPIDP), and the Province of British Columbia through the British Columbia Arts Council for their support of its publishing program.

National Library of Canada Cataloguing in Publication Data
Beveridge, Cathy
    Shadows of disaster / Cathy Beveridge.

    ISBN 978-1-55380-002-6 (print)
    ISBN 978-1-55380-287-7 (ebook) / ISBN 978-1-55380-286-0 (pdf)

    I. Frank (Alta.) — History — Landslide, 1903 — Juvenile fiction. I. Title.
PS8553.E897S52 2003   jC813'.6   C2002-911116-1
PZ7.B4684Sh 2003

*For my grandmother,
Mamie Basso, who told me
stories in the shadow
of Frank Slide.*

ACKNOWLEDGEMENTS

I would like to thank Monica Field of the Frank Slide Interpretive Centre for her assistance in ensuring historical accuracy and Dr. Michael Slawinski and Dr. Yves Rogister for
sharing their scientific expertise. I am grateful for the feed-
back and encouragement of the 2001 Sagehill Writing Young
Adult Fiction Group: Kevin Major, Sheena Koops, Curtis
Parkinson, Diane Salmon, Arthur Slade and Joan Weir.

Every attempt has been made to preserve the historical
accuracy of the events surrounding Frank Slide. While the
characters are based on many different actual people, they
have all been fictionalized — out of respect for those whose
ancestors were affected by the slide.

Chapter One

Jolene felt the colour flush her cheeks, spread around the contours of her chin and creep down her neck. Her teacher's words swirled around her ears. She stole a glance across the classroom at Michael, her twin brother. He was digging his thumbnail into the nicked edge of the desk as if he hadn't seen what Mrs. Perkins was holding.

"This summer," said Mrs. Perkins holding up a pile of turquoise coupons, "Jolene and Michael's father will be opening his new Museum of Disasters. Most of you will recall his visit to our class a few weeks ago." A snicker escaped from the back of the room.

Jolene closed her eyes, trying *not* to recall that exact same visit. Dad had been so excited about showing them the height of the flames that had burned some local grain elevator decades ago that he had fallen off Mrs. Perkins' chair and landed spread-eagled on her desk.

"Mr. Fortini has kindly donated coupons good for one free visit to his museum for each student in this class." Mrs. Perkins' voice was on the move, coming in her direction. It stopped directly beside her. Jolene opened one eye and saw turquoise. "Would you like to pass them out please, Jolene?"

Painfully aware of her crimson face, Jolene rose slowly to her feet. Taking the coupons from her teacher's hand, she began placing them on the corner of each desk. She held her breath as she set one on Gerard's desk, then moved quickly to the next row.

Rachel picked up her coupon and read the printed message aloud. "Relive the disasters that many did not live through."

Curtis curled his between his fingertips. "Watch the flames leap into the sky like a dragon's breath," he proclaimed, mimicking her father.

"See the waters surge at the speed of light," quipped Cory.

Jolene tried not to listen, tried not to hear. Michael gave her a sympathetic smile as she returned to her desk, her hands empty.

"And now, before you leave for holidays — report cards!" exclaimed Mrs. Perkins, dropping a creamy envelope on Jolene's desk. Jolene slid the long sheet imprinted with the school logo out of the envelope. She scanned it quickly, then slipped it back inside as the bell rang. "Have a wonderful summer. And good luck in grade seven," their teacher called after them.

Outside, Jolene said her summertime goodbyes and headed for home. In past years, when school let out, she and Michael had raced the whole way, anticipating the freedom of late mornings, campouts in their fort, and best of all, beachcombing with their cousins on the west coast. But today she didn't feel like running. She didn't feel like celebrating.

She heard the thumping of Michael's feet as he ran to catch up with her. "Hey JoJo," he called, using the childhood name that he still used when they were alone, "wait up." Jolene slowed. Michael fell into step beside her, his dark wavy hair bouncing into place. He stared at her with the deep green eyes they had both inherited from their grandfather. "What's wrong?" he asked, catching sight of her long face. "Bad report card?"

It was a dumb thought, but then Michael was given to dumb thoughts on occasion. "Straight A's. How about you?"

"Well," he said brightly, "I got a B in language arts, and a B in social studies."

That was pretty good for Michael. He always had difficulty with the subjects that required a lot of writing.

"And I got an A in math," he announced proudly, a long grin joining his dimples.

Jolene's eyes widened in surprise. Normally Michael got B's in math. Once, last year, he'd even had a C. "But I thought you . . . how'd you pull off an A?"

Michael's grin threatened to overrun his dimples. "Mr. Saunders gave me extra marks for going in that math competition — the one he wanted you to enter. Remember?"

Jolene remembered. Mr. Saunders had wanted her to represent the school in an interschool math competition. She'd declined, but Michael had entered it. And Mr. Saunders had given him extra marks for competing, extra marks for an extracurricular activity. That was hardly fair.

"You should have done it, Jo. I bet you'd have won the math award if you had."

Jolene felt her shoulders tighten. The math award had gone to Jeannette Stevens and now Jolene knew why. She'd been positive that she would win it. After all, she'd beat Jeannette on every test but one and she'd had near-perfect marks on all her assignments.

She remembered sitting in the gymnasium on awards night, feeling her heart speed up as Mr. Saunders took the microphone. She'd taken care to smooth the wrinkles out of her skirt and ensure that her sandals were buckled so that she wouldn't trip going up the steps to the stage. Mr. Saunders had given the usual prologue. "This year, the math award goes to an outstanding student, a girl who is always ready to take on a new mathematical challenge. I am delighted to call on this year's award recipient . . . Jeannette Stevens." Jeannette Stevens? Jolene had actually been in the process of pushing herself up out of her chair. Jeannette Stevens? How had it happened?

Now she knew. Jeannette had participated in the math

competition. Jolene kicked at a bottle cap and sent it clattering onto the road. She hated those contests — you never knew what they were going to ask you or if you were going to make a fool of yourself in front of all those people. Things like that didn't bother Michael so much. He was more like Dad.

"Dad shouldn't have handed out those coupons," said Jolene, her speech following her thoughts.

"Why? Don't you think anybody will go?"

"They might, but I'm not sure that they should." Michael looked up at her, confusion in his eyes. "We went to the museum last weekend while you were away at your swim meet," said Jolene.

"And what's wrong with it?"

Jolene scraped her shoe along a crack in the sidewalk, remembering the displays. Huge, brilliant photographs lined the walls as backdrops. Artifacts, carefully dated and explained, were everywhere. And yet there was something missing. "It's so, so . . . dead," she said finally. "It reminds me of social studies class."

"Then he'll never make a go of it."

"I know," said Jolene. "That's the whole point." Two years ago, Dad had given up his job as an engineer to work on his museum so that he could help preserve history. At first, she and Michael had loved the idea of putting fires, massacres, floods and mudslides on exhibit. But that was turning out to be much harder than any of them had thought. "He should have never started it."

Michael's eyes registered his surprise. "But it's always been his dream. He loves history. I guess he inherited that from Gramps."

Jolene wasn't so sure. It was true that her grandfather loved to read about history and that he told stories about the past, but he wasn't like Dad at all. Grandpa's stories were funny and interesting and captivating. She and Michael had been listening to them for as long as Jolene could remember. Stories for bedtime, stories for special occasions, stories for no reason at all. "It's different with Dad," she said, a hint of irritation in her voice. "He gets all caught up in the details. You know — the way he marks Louis Riel's birthday in his day timer or plants a bean seed for every one of the victims of the Cypress Hills Massacre every year. It's strange."

Michael did not reply.

His silence bugged her. "He's going to end up looking like a fool when this Museum of Disaster opens." Jolene kicked at a loose pebble. "I wouldn't do it if I were him," she said. "It's going to be so embarrassing."

"Maybe," Michael said thoughtfully as they reached the driveway of their house, "but I guess when something's really important to you, you have to take that risk."

Jolene's response was drowned out by the sound of Dad's rusty pick-up truck. "Hey!" he called out the open window. "Look what I found today." He reached across the front seat and held up an old, sooty lantern.

"Good one," called Michael.

Dad started towards the house, clutching the lantern close to his chest like a child having rediscovered a broken toy at the bottom of his toy box. Black streaks stained Dad's shirt and hands, but he didn't notice. "This lantern is very interesting," he said aloud to nobody in particular. "It was first used in . . . " He disappeared inside the house.

"See what I mean," Jolene told Michael.

"Yeah," he agreed following his father with his eyes, but his face was lost in a boyish grin.

"Here's to two great report cards," said Grandpa, raising his water glass after Mom had served up supper.

Mom smiled. "It's nice to see that math mark come up, son." Mom was a professor in the Department of Mathematics and Statistics at the university. Glasses clinked all around. Jolene waited for Mom to say something about her marks, but there was only silence. Had Mom forgotten that she'd got an A in math and every other subject as a final grade? That she'd brought home straight A's in math all year? She took a sip of water. Or maybe Mom had just come to expect it.

"And here's to successful seasons of swimming and gymnastics," said Dad, proposing another toast.

"Yes," agreed Mom. "You both did very well, but I'm certainly glad it's over for a while. All that driving about."

Again they clinked glasses. Jolene raised her glass, but did not touch the lip of her glass to her father's. Had it been an intentional slight? An attempt to humiliate her? She sawed intensely at her chicken breast.

"Here's to that silver medal," Dad said, toasting Michael.

Michael smiled, excitement flooding his face. "It was that suicide turn," he said, his eyes sparkling. Last weekend at provincials, he had swum a 200 metre individual medley race and had opted for the faster, but more dangerous suicide turn going from backstroke to breaststroke, rather than the traditional one. The top four finishers had been within three tenths of a second of each other's times. Michael had managed to walk away with a silver medal, even though he hadn't been one of the top three going into the race. Jolene didn't begrudge Michael his success. It was Dad and what he *wasn't* saying that was getting under her skin. She stabbed at the cucumber on her plate.

"And you had a very good gymnastics season, too."

Dad's words fell heavily across the table. Jolene did not look up. Her fingers clenched the handle of her fork. A *very good* season! He may as well have come right out and called it mediocre. Anyway that was the truth, especially compared to her previous year. After her third-place all-around showing last year, her sixth-place finish this year had been dismal and they all knew it.

"Next year will be better, when you nail all those aerials," said Michael encouragingly.

Would it? Would it be better? Jolene wondered. Her

coach had wanted her to raise the level of difficulty in her routines this year. He'd warned her that she'd need to add some tricks and Jolene had worked hard to master them and had, for the most part. But when it had come to the actual performance, she hadn't been able to bring herself to put them in. Instead she'd opted for safe, easier, clean routines. Good enough for sixth place.

Grandpa wiped his bushy moustache with his napkin. "And here's to all of you for having to live with a surly old man," he said, raising his glass.

"Hear, hear," said Dad jokingly.

Jolene clinked glasses with her grandfather. That was the only good thing that had happened lately. Her grandfather had come to stay at their place a few weeks ago, but even that was shrouded in mystery and suspicion.

"Your grandfather is ill," Mom had told her when she'd asked why he was moving in.

"Ill? He can throw a baseball farther than any of the kids in my class," she had protested.

"Illness comes in many forms," her mother had said, curtly dismissing her as if she were a little girl.

So far, she hadn't seen any indication of illness although Grandpa did make some strange comments occasionally and sometimes he seemed very tired. But Mom had refused to talk about it. Jolene scowled at her mother, her insides churning.

Dad was talking about the museum again. He was always

talking about the museum. She ground her teeth and spread the rice out on her plate so her parents wouldn't notice that she hadn't eaten it. The conversation drifted to the dimensions of Dad's lantern. Jolene stabbed at the tomatoes in her salad as the discussion turned to handles and hooks. She had a sudden urge to scream, to holler at the top of her lungs, to drown out her father's words. She stuffed a forkful of chicken into her mouth and chewed fiercely. Dad launched into an explanation of wicks and string and Jolene felt a sudden, inexplicable urge to cry. She pushed her chair back and jumped to her feet. The conversation stopped. All eyes stared at her.

"Can I be excused?" she muttered.

"Sure, I guess," said Dad. "But don't forget that you have to pack tonight. I'd like to get away by mid-morning tomorrow so that we can be in the Crowsnest Pass in time for my appointment." His gaze shifted to Grandpa. "You too, Dad."

Jolene tried not to let Dad's words register on her brain. She couldn't. If they did, she knew she would either cry or scream. She hurried to the sink, scraped her leftover food into the garbage and opened the dishwasher.

"And when do you leave for your conference?" Dad asked Mom.

"Sunday night. But Michael flies tomorrow at 2:45." Tears welled in Jolene's eyes. She blinked, tried to concentrate instead on sliding her plate between the short blue plastic prongs. She couldn't bear to hear what she knew would come next. "Make sure you take everything you need for swim camp, Michael, as well as stuff for the beach."

A tear slipped from the corner of her eye. She brushed it angrily away and kept her head bowed below the counter. Michael was so lucky. He'd been chosen for a select swim camp in Vancouver, but before that, he was going to stay a week with their cousins. Another tear followed the path of the first one. Jolene rearranged the glasses in the dishwasher, not wanting to look up.

Michael joined her at the sink, scraped his plate and placed it beside hers, his movements replicas of hers. "Couldn't Jo fly out with me for the week at Aunt Robyn's?" he asked as if he could sense her despair.

Jolene looked up hopefully. If only she could escape from here for a week. If only she could race down the sand with the wind and salty mist blowing in her face.

Dad sighed. "Not this year, I'm afraid. We've had to dip into our savings quite a bit lately what with the swimming and gymnastics and all; it's tough right now. Your way is paid for, Michael, so that's different." He took a deep breath. "Once the museum is open, things will be better. Besides," he said encouragingly, "there's lots to see in the Crowsnest Pass, including a huge rock slide and lots of old coal mining stuff. We'll have fun, won't we, Jolene?"

"Sure," she said closing the dishwasher with a thud.

She left the kitchen with Michael at her heels. "Want to

go to the fort?" he asked. They had not been there for many months, but as children, it had been the site of many treasured moments — pirate games, secret codes, amateur vet schools.

"No thanks."

"Remember when we found that magpie that had been attacked by a cat and you nursed it back to health? And then it tried to attack you when you wanted to release it."

Jolene smiled at her brother's efforts to cheer her. "Thanks, Michael," she said, meaning it, "but I'd better go pack." He did not try to dissuade her.

Upstairs, she closed her door, dragged the suitcase out from underneath her bed and started transferring clothes from her drawers to her luggage. Three weeks ago, before Michael had been selected for the swim camp, they had both intended to go with Dad. Back then she had almost been looking forward to this trip. But now the idea of trying to amuse herself in an old coal mining town on the edge of a big rock slide left her feeling forlorn and empty. She pulled a handful of books off her shelf and stuffed them into her suitcase. She wasn't even sure how long they'd be gone. It all depended on Dad's research. She added an extra pair of shorts and two tank tops to her neat piles of colour. At least her grandfather would be there.

Her suitcase packed, Jolene flopped down on her stomach on her bed. She perched on her elbows and slid her hands under the pillow. Silent tears trickled down her cheeks.

So many things had changed this year. Even Michael had changed, she thought, recalling their conversation on the way home from school. Two wet patches formed on her pillowcase. And things had changed at home, too. This year, it was as if Michael's accomplishments meant more than hers.

Jolene picked up a framed picture of herself and Michael on the beach last summer. Sure, she was a few minutes older and he was a few centimetres taller, but they were remarkably similar — same hair, same eyes, same features. Their teachers always remarked on their many similarities — or at least they had in the past.

Jolene got to her feet and paced about her room. It wasn't fair that Michael got to go to Vancouver when she didn't. Dad had blamed their money problems on her gymnastics and Michael's swimming, but it wasn't their fault. It was because he'd quit his job to open this stupid museum that they were strapped for money.

She reached for her brush and gave her hair a few vigorous strokes. Then throwing open the door, she strode into the hallway. She marched from room to room, looking for something, but not knowing what. Finally, she picked up a magazine about ocean life and went out onto the front verandah to sit on the swing. Bottle-nosed dolphins jumped through the pages, but her mind could not follow them. She was too much on edge — taut, stretched, strained.

Rusty splinters of sunlight stuck up from the horizon. She dug her bare toes into the wooden boards of the porch and pushed. Back and forth, back and forth she swung, trying to shake her thoughts loose. Eyes closed, she pushed and swung.

"May I join you?" Her grandfather stood beside the swing, twirling his moustache.

She halted at the lowest point and he eased himself onto the cushions. Jolene pushed off with her toes again. Back and forth. Back and forth.

"Tough day?" asked Grandpa. It was, Jolene knew, his way of inviting her to talk. She said nothing, but continued to swing, pushing and pulling her thoughts. Copper rays lingered on the horizon.

"Why does life have to get so complicated?" she asked finally. Grandpa waited. "Last year, things were so much simpler."

"Were they?"

"Well, school seemed easier," she said softly.

Grandpa tilted his head and regarded her curiously. "Straight A's is pretty good."

"And gymnastics was easier last year, too." Jolene pushed off and raised her feet, letting the swing go at its own pace. The streetlights blinked on and off, as if trying to decide if they were needed yet. "At least Michael had a good year," she said dismally.

Grandpa nodded his head. "You both had a good year. Michael took some chances and they worked out for him. Sometimes it's good to take a risk."

Jolene didn't respond. Michael had said something similar on the way home from school and for some reason that thought left her feeling uneasy.

"Take your father, for instance. For the last decade, he's been talking about opening a Museum of Disasters. Even when he was working as an engineer, he was reading, going to sales and auctions, writing away for information. Then a couple of years ago, he decided to quit his job and devote his time to making the museum a reality. He took a big risk."

Jolene pushed off hard with her toes. "A risk that's never going to amount to anything." She softened her tone. "I know Dad's put a lot of effort into this museum, but what are the chances of it succeeding? You've seen it."

"It's not finished yet," said Grandpa guardedly. "Your dad's done a lot of research. People are intrigued by disasters and he thinks there's a market for it." The swing slowed.

"If it doesn't work, he's going to look like such a fool. We're all going to look like fools."

Grandpa stood up, the swing rocking swiftly. "There's worse things than looking like a fool," he replied. "And sometimes having the courage to try is more important than not failing."

His words brushed over her and left her skin tingling. If she'd competed in the interschool math competition, she might have won the math award. Then again, she might have blown it completely. And perhaps, if she'd elected to do some of her big aerials, she'd have scored higher in her gymnastics competition. That was, of course, if she hadn't fallen on her face.

"Not everyone's a risk-taker," said Grandpa.

"Michael is."

"Maybe more so than you. And it's not good to be foolish about taking risks, but you can learn to take risks. I did."

Dad and Grandpa had learned to do it and so had Michael. Why hadn't she been able to take some risks this year? Jolene pressed her fingertips together. "Maybe it's easier when you're a boy," she said suddenly. She wasn't sure where the thought had come from, but it made sense to her. She jumped off the swing and joined her grandfather at the porch railing. "People expect boys to be risk-takers, to do courageous things and take chances. They don't expect girls to do those things, so we don't." Her voice rang through the dusk.

"I'm not sure about that," said Grandpa. "Look at all the courageous women in history — Laura Secord, Nellie McClung."

Jolene only half heard his words. "It's easier if you're male," she said. "I wish I were a boy like Michael." It was out of her mouth before she'd realized she'd said it.

Grandpa chuckled. "You've been telling us that ever since you were a little tyke. Except back then, your mother liked to tie your hair back and you wanted to be a boy so you could wear it short like Michael did."

"Like Michael did what?" asked Michael, joining them on the verandah.

"We were just discussing the advantage you have being male," said Jolene boldly. "How it's easier for you to be a risk-taker because you're a boy."

Michael plunked down on the swing. He pushed off with his bare toes. Back and forth. Back and forth. "What does being a boy or being a girl have to do with taking risks?"

"Jo believes that boys become greater risk-takers because society expects them to be more courageous and rambunctious," explained Grandpa.

"Maybe, but I think it has more to do with personality. There's always a chance that you'll screw up and look like an idiot when you take a risk. I guess it depends how much that matters to you."

Jolene pushed that thought from her mind with a fierce shove. "If I were a boy, I'd have gone in that math contest," she proclaimed. "And I'd have done all those aerials in competition, too." The idea carried her away. "If I were a boy, I'd do all kinds of things — take drama, run for student council, ride saddle broncs, bungee jump, all kinds of stuff."

Michael inclined his head towards Grandpa. "What's got into her tonight?" he asked, standing up and stretching through the night air.

Grandpa adjusted the suspenders he always wore, put his arms around their shoulders and steered them towards the front door. "It's too late in the day for this heavy thinking," he said. "Goodnight, both of you."

Upstairs, Jolene pushed open her window and stood looking out at the glittering sky. Mars, the red planet, was visible tonight. Many of the planets had been named for mythological gods — Mars, Pluto, Mercury. Warriors, rebels, messengers — all risk-takers and all males. It was easier to be brave and courageous when you were a boy. It really was.

Chapter Two

Michael was lucky. He'd been born a boy. Jolene was still mulling over that thought as she stumbled down the stairs the next morning, her suitcase in tow. If only they'd been identical twins — but there was no sense wishing those wishes.

She hauled her suitcase through the door and set it on the porch. Her parents weren't in sight, but their voices reached her from the driveway.

"You've seen him, staring into space, twirling his moustache and telling those bizarre stories about things he's never seen." Mom's voice.

Jolene pressed herself against the wall of the house, out of sight of her parents, and listened. They were, she knew, talking about her grandfather. She held her breath as Mom continued.

"Yesterday, two of the neighbours met him down by the river and he told them that he'd almost been washed away in the flood on Monday. We haven't had a drop of rain for weeks."

"He obviously isn't feeling well." Dad's voice.

"He isn't well. His mind is deteriorating." Jolene crept closer. "I know it's not easy, Rod, but we can't ignore it. After all, there is a history of senility in your family."

Senility? The word throbbed in Jolene's head.

"Remember your great aunt Peggy?"

Aunt Peggy? Who was this great aunt Peggy and what did her being senile have to do with Grandpa?

There was a moment of silence before Dad responded. "Do you think he could be ill with the same thing?"

Jolene didn't want to hear anymore. She lugged her suitcase noisily down the steps and threw her backpack in the backseat without looking up. "Where's Gramps?" she asked finally, staring hard at her parents.

Her father glanced quickly at her mother. "He's on the ridge," he replied gently. "Would you mind looking for him, Jolene? We have to go very shortly. I have an appointment at 2:30."

Jolene followed her feet to the ridge overlooking the Bow River. Her mother's words blew over the grasses. They dulled the wild pinkness of the rose and muffled the call of the robin. Mom couldn't be right. Grandpa wasn't senile. There were times when he acted a little strange, but that didn't mean he was crazy. She broke into a trot thinking of her conversation with Grandpa last night. She'd had dozens of similar conversations with him over the years. He was fine, just fine!

Grandpa's polished, wooden bench was just in front of her, but he was nowhere in sight. Jolene ducked into the shadow of an overhanging branch. The lilac bushes whispered and she jumped. "Gramps!" She caught her breath. "You scared me. What are you doing hiding in the bushes?"

He raised one hand. "Be careful. Follow the path of Running Bear's moccasins."

Jolene stared hard at her grandfather. What was he doing? And why today of all days? "Come on, Gramps, let's go. Dad's got the car packed."

"There are many buffalo. Already, I can feel the ground tremble beneath my feet." Grandpa moved towards the trailhead. A dark cloud shadowed the sun. "You must hurry or they will be upon you. Go quickly. Running Bear is waiting for you."

The wind gusted and Jolene shivered. "Gramps, cut it out!" The fear in her voice surprised her. "I don't know any Running Bear and . . . "

"Dust." Her grandfather raised one hand to shade his eyes and looked past her towards the houses on the ridge. He took her hand and pulled her towards the trail, but Jolene dug her heels into the soft earth.

"Gramps!" She grabbed his arm and shook it. "Stop it!"

She leaned towards him, her mother's words racing through the sky. "Stop it!"

His body jolted and went limp. She staggered under his weight. Slowly, gasping for breath, her grandfather raised his head. "Jo." He steadied himself. "It's you."

Jolene's body trembled as his weight shifted away from her. "Of course it's me," she managed.

Grandpa took a deep breath and straightened up slowly. "I guess we should go."

Just like that? Without a word of explanation? Jolene wiped the sweat from her forehead and tried to keep the anxiety out of her voice. "Dad's waiting for you."

"Always a problem, I am." Grandpa smiled fondly at her.

It was the same fond smile he always gave her, and yet somehow different today. Jolene studied her grandfather's weathered face. His green eyes, so much like hers and Michael's, were empty and distant now. She swerved to miss a tiny grasshopper and fell into step beside him. A wave of sunshine washed over the grasses. He'd been playing around, making up a story — that was all.

But her uncertainty persisted with each one of Grandpa's silent steps. She ran her fingers up the stems of the grasses, and drew up her courage. "You really had me going back there. I've never heard that story about Running Bear before."

Grandpa stopped. "It wasn't a story, Jo. Running Bear was a real person and those cliffs used to be a buffalo jump." He looked into her eyes and suddenly Jolene was afraid.

"Jolene, your mom's looking for you." The little boy she sometimes babysat called from across the field.

Jolene didn't move. She stood riveted to the ground like the large pine tree in front of her.

Grandpa dropped his eyes. "My fault," he called. "I didn't notice the time. I guess we should be going."

Jolene said nothing as they drove south through Calgary, but she could not push her mother's words from her head. Dad interrupted her thoughts. "Once we get to the Crowsnest Pass, a lady by the name of Karen will be taking us around to the big rock slide, the interpretive centre, the old coal mine and some other sites. I need some good photos for the museum exhibit, so there should be lots of time for sightseeing."

Jolene scowled at Dad. Rocks and coal! Not exactly her idea of a fun summer vacation. It was bad enough knowing that Michael would be building sand creatures, collecting crabs and body surfing, but it was even worse knowing that she was being dragged into Dad's pointless quest to preserve history.

"Look," said Grandpa, holding up the newspaper. "Here's a write-up about some of the museums in town."

Behind the wheel, Dad jumped. The car swerved dangerously into the lane beside them. "Is my museum there?" he asked. "I showed the reporter around last week."

Jolene studied the paper over her grandfather's shoulder as he skimmed the article. "Museum of Disasters," read

Grandpa aloud. "Rod Fortini has tackled an interesting concept — the preservation of destruction. Fortini must be commended for his attention to detail, evident in carefully labelled artifacts and panoramic photographs." Dad smiled broadly. Jolene could see her grandfather hesitate before continuing. "However, there is little feel for the hearts and souls of those who suffered and perished. Hopefully, Fortini will find a way to add this dimension to a museum that has the potential to be an intriguing means of preserving history." Grandpa closed the paper.

"Little feel for the hearts and souls of those who suffered and perished," echoed Dad. "How is anybody supposed to do that?"

Jolene said nothing. She stared at her reflection in the car window as they emerged from Calgary, pressed her headphones into her ears and cranked up her music. She didn't want to think about it — not Dad's museum, Mom's ideas, Michael's good luck or Grandpa's strange behaviour — none of it. She closed her eyes and leaned back against the window, thinking instead of Gerard.

Gerard, with his dark, thick curls and his warm, slow smile that uncurled like a lazy caterpillar in the sun. It had been one of the last days of school and they had been cleaning out the storage cupboard at the back of the classroom. They hadn't said much, just stood side by side constructing piles of colours, sorting scribblers and feeling a dusty nearness. And when the cupboard was empty, he'd smiled at her and asked her if she ever swam at the Silver Springs out-door pool. His brother would be life guarding there, so he planned to go often this summer. She'd nodded, unable to trust her voice. And now? Now the pool and Gerard had been replaced by rocks and coal and disasters.

She pulled her headphones off and reached for the CD case. Grandpa's voice broke the silence. "I've often won-dered what my grandfather must have thought when he arrived here from Italy with his family." They had turned west off the main highway and were driving into the foothills. "I wonder what went through his mind as he trav-elled this way towards the Pass."

"How long did he live in the Crowsnest Pass?" Dad asked.

"They arrived a few months before the slide. Afterwards, my grandmother wanted to leave."

"Was she scared that the mountain would slide again?" asked Dad.

Grandpa shrugged. "Maybe, but it was just a few weeks after the slide that Peggy disappeared."

Jolene leaned forward. "What happened to your aunt Peggy?"

"No one really knows for sure." Grandpa chose his words carefully. "Apparently she was an intelligent girl who en-joyed long conversations with her father. He'd been a scien-tist in Italy. One day Peggy went out into the forest and came back talking about strange things she'd seen that didn't actually exist."

"And then she went missing?" asked Dad.

"She did. They found her shawl near the river. Most folks assumed that she'd drowned."

Jolene swallowed hard. "Was she sick mentally?"

Grandpa sighed and Dad watched him out of the corner of his eye. "Maybe. Who knows?" he said finally.

Maybe, and maybe Grandpa had inherited it. Jolene turned the diskman back on, closed her eyes and let the music drift through her.

BLACK DIAMOND read the sign when she opened her eyes. On the shoulder, at the only intersection in town, two cowboys slept in the cab of a truck, their hats pulled down to their chins. Furtive eyes peered through the slats of the horse trailer. Didn't crazy people's eyes go wild and frenzied? Grandpa's eyes weren't like that.

Grandpa had closed his eyes and leaned his head back against the headrest. Jolene stared out at the grassy hills, divided only by an occasional swath of trees or a reluctant creek. Clouds, like sheepskin rugs, lay in the sky as they approached the town of Longview. And it was a long view, down the valley, through the rolling foothills all the way to the curtain of mountains in the west. An upside-down birdhouse hung from a fencepost and Jolene wondered if the birds had even noticed that it was upside-down. Surely they would have noticed anything that wasn't green. The entire valley was a quilt of green — a lime green patch of grass, a dark green patch of pine, a fresh green patch of barley, a shimmering green patch of poplar leaves — all stitched together with the silver thread of the creek. The creek rolled and dipped, disappeared and reappeared until, suddenly, the lakes surfaced. "Chain Lakes," called her Dad, through her music.

A few minutes later, Dad screeched to a stop and Jolene felt her seatbelt grip her. Ahead, four large, fluttering birds rushed about on the pavement, following the dotted yellow line before disappearing in a flap into the opposite ditch. Jolene pulled the headphones from her ears. "Wild turkeys!" exclaimed Grandpa, jolting awake. "I haven't seen them for ages."

The car rolled slowly forward. Grandpa pointed to a dark bank of clouds that hung threateningly above the mountains, their shadows descending to the earth. "Looks like a storm brewing through the Pass."

"Think so?" asked Dad, squinting.

Grandpa glanced back at Jolene. "Did you bring your kite, Jo?"

"No. Should I have?"

"It's always windy in the Crowsnest Pass," Grandpa told her. Outside the car, the prairie grasses slanted sharply. "I remember one wind during the depression years. What a wind that was! Nick — I think his name was — was walking home late one night. He came around this bluff and the wind, she was a howlin' like a pack of hungry wolves. So he tucked himself into a narrow trail alongside the railway tracks where the trees and cliffs gave him some shelter. Well, if a train didn't come along. With that wind howling, it created an air drag so fierce, it almost sucked him right under the wheels. When he came into town, his hair was standing straight on end in big tufts, his hands were all cut up and bleeding from trying to hang onto the rocky cliffs and his eyes had gone all cross-eyed. His hands healed up and his hair got put back into place, but his eyes never did go back. The wind had crossed 'em something bad — so bad that when he cried, the tears rolled down his back."

Jolene laughed aloud.

"But you never lived there." Dad's face wrinkled skeptically.

Jolene cringed. Mom's words howled in her ears and Grandpa twirled his moustache. The rain hit. He couldn't be going crazy — not like her best friend's grandmother who was always seeing little men on the windowsill and imagining that her nightgowns had been redone as armchair covers. But still, Grandpa had told that story as if he'd been there.

The windshield wipers attacked the raindrops. Dad turned the car west and studied Grandpa's profile. "Marilyn's really worried about you," Dad told Grandpa. Jolene held her breath. "Lately you seem to be . . . " A gust of wind rocked the car. Dad fought to regain control. "Sometimes, you seem rather confused about . . . " A big semi-trailer truck passed on the opposite side of the road, flooding the windows with water. Dad gripped the steering wheel tightly, searching frantically for the road. For a moment, Jolene could see nothing except water and the swishing wipers. Then suddenly, patches of yellow appeared, directly in front of them. Dad swerved back into his lane. He held tightly to the wheel, his knuckles bold and bony. "I hope we drive out of this soon," he muttered.

In the backseat, Jolene exhaled slowly. A gust of wind had blown the idea of her grandfather's senility away for now, but the wind wouldn't continue forever.

As they rounded a bend, lightning flashed, lighting up a weathered tree, its branches outstretched like the limbs of a bony dancer, its trunk thrust into the wind.

"That's the crooked tree," said Grandpa. "I read that it's been petrified by the wind and rain. It means we're almost there."

Jolene struggled to read the sign outside her window: MUNICIPALITY OF CROWSNEST PASS. On her right, an enormous crow perching on a wooden nest marked the turnoff to the town of Bellevue.

"Bellevue," read Dad. "It sounds French. What's it mean, Jolene?"

"Beautiful view," said Jolene, drawing on her years of French immersion at school. "Except right now, there's no view."

It was true. The clouds were socked in all around them. They drove down mainstreet with its few sad buildings.

What was she going to do here in this old coal mining town? She peered through the rain-streaked windows, able only to distinguish the signs of the Pass Dairy and Bellevue Post Office.

"Frank Slide is just west of us, under those clouds," Dad told Jolene as they turned onto the crest of a hill overlooking the highway. "That's where the old town of Frank used to be, at the base of Turtle Mountain." Jolene squinted through the rain, but could see nothing. "And here's our house." Dad stopped in front of the small, blue house he had rented.

Clutching their luggage, they darted to the porch. The door was unlocked. Jolene and Grandpa went in to explore the house while Dad fetched the remaining bags from the car. Then he rushed off to his appointment.

Jolene took her time unpacking. Her bedroom, strong with the scent of lemon furniture polish, was painted the yellow of buffalo beans. Listening to the distant thunder, she put her clothes away in the dresser, hung up her coat and arranged the contents of her backpack on the night table. She could hear Grandpa moving about in the living room.

She ran a brush through her short hair. People often said they looked alike, she and Grandpa — the same green eyes, the same smile. Mom even said they thought the same way. Jolene frowned. She wished she could think like him now, figure out why he was acting so weird.

Jolene joined her grandfather at the window. "Gramps," she began uncertainly, "can I ask you a question?"

"Sure Jo."

"Back there on the ridge today before we left, did you really think Running Bear was . . . ?" Her voice trailed off. Grandpa gazed out the window.

"I mean, they're stories, right? It's all that historic stuff you read, and the way you love to tell stories, isn't it?"

"I do love to tell stories," said Grandpa evenly.

"That's what I thought." Jolene breathed a sigh of relief.

Grandpa looked thoughtfully at her. "You could see me when I spoke to you about Running Bear, couldn't you?"

Jolene looked puzzled. "Of course I could see you. What kind of question is that? I'm not the . . . "

"Crazy one," concluded Grandpa sadly.

Jolene sighed. "You *were* just telling stories, weren't you?"

Grandpa stayed silent. Jolene wished he would say something, anything. "Do you want the truth?" he asked finally.

She nodded quickly before she could change her mind.

Grandpa drew a long breath. "The first time it happened," he began, "I was scared, too." He gave Jolene a lopsided grin. "I was in eastern Alberta on the prairies, visiting an old school friend. It was a gorgeous day, one of those days where the wheat holds up the sun and sky and I'd gone out for a walk. But it was hotter than I reckoned and I soon found myself heading for the shade of a nearby stand of trees. The shadows were deep and thick and I stepped into them anticipating a cool repose. But the air in the shadows was hot and tangible. Everything went black and I lost my balance. It felt like I was being pulled apart. Then suddenly, the pressure was gone and when I looked up, a fire was raging across the plains just like it did in 1909."

Jolene stared at the lined face beside her, trying to read her grandfather's eyes. "1909?"

"Yes, Jo. I've found a way to go back in time, to step back into history."

Jolene gazed out the window, tears cresting in her eyes. He really was crazy.

"I'm not crazy," Grandpa laughed as if he'd read her mind. "Even if it sounds like I am. And I'm not the only one in the family who's ever travelled through time either."

"Aunt Peggy?" asked Jolene flatly.

Grandpa chuckled. "Yes, poor Aunt Peggy and her father and maybe others."

Raising her eyebrows, Jolene flopped down into a chair. Just her luck, she was descended from a whole line of lunatics.

"My grandfather, Peggy's father, wrote about it in his journal," explained Grandpa. Jolene stared absently ahead. "He was trained as a physicist in Italy and he had this theory about time being continuous and . . ." His voice trailed off as he moved towards Jolene's chair. "I know it's tough to understand, Jo."

"No kidding," muttered Jolene.

"But it is possible."

"Abracadabra, alakazoom and poof you're back in time?"

Grandpa grinned. "Not quite like that. I go back through time creases."

"Time creases?" she echoed skeptically. This was even worse than she'd imagined. "So then, today, on the ridge . . . you thought you were watching a buffalo hunt?"

Grandpa nodded. "Those old hills overlooking the river used to be a buffalo jump. There's a time crease right beside that lilac bush by my bench."

"Really?" she said, aware of the slight mocking tone in her voice. "I've never noticed."

Grandpa winced. "I know it's hard to believe, Jo. It's hard for me, too."

So why did he believe it then? Why didn't he just stop? "You can't just go through some time crease and end up back in history someplace."

"But I do."

Couldn't he hear how crazy he sounded? "But today, you could see me and I wasn't in the past."

"That happens sometimes. Time gets crossed over and I get all mixed up."

Jolene looked out the window. She pressed her fingers together, her thoughts racing with the thinning clouds. Tears trickled down her cheeks. It was no wonder that Mom was worried. With an aching heart, Jolene watched her grandfather sip his cup of coffee.

Grandpa held up his cup in front of the window. "Look at that, will you. Frank Slide!"

Jolene looked up. The clouds had blown off and ahead of her stretched an enormous slide of fallen boulders. She gazed up at Turtle Mountain, half its face gone, its rocky cheekbones shattered.

Chapter Three

Karen arrived early the next morning to take them on the Bellevue coal mine tour. "Rocks and coal," muttered Jolene. "Everywhere you look, rocks and coal."

Karen stopped the car at the bottom of the winding road that descended to the Bellevue mine and they clambered out. To the west, they could see Frank Slide — ninety million tons of rock that had buried the mine and part of the town of Frank in 1903. But it was coal, according to Karen, that had been the soul of the Crowsnest Pass. And it was from the mines like this one, scattered throughout the Pass, that the coal had been taken.

Karen disappeared inside a nearby building and rejoined them a few minutes later, carrying four battery packs and headlamps. She showed them how to adjust the packs on their waists and click on the headlamps attached to their yellow hardhats. Jolene glanced at Grandpa. He almost looked like a miner, but that wasn't really surprising. Even though he'd never lived or worked in the Crowsnest Pass, he had worked in the mines in northern Alberta years ago. She didn't want to think about how foolish she looked.

Instead, Jolene wandered towards the entrance of the mine and peered inside. To the left of her stretched a tunnel of night. To the right stood an old wooden cart. Grandpa, Dad and Karen joined her shortly.

"The Bellevue mine was in operation from 1903 until 1962," Karen told them, moving towards the wooden cart. "This main tunnel or gangway is where the coal cars, like this one, came out." Karen ran a hand over the oily surface of the cart. "The cars were pulled out of the mine by big draft horses. Most of them could pull seven cars at one time. They pulled them to the tipple, where they were tipped over and the rocks were removed by hand on the picking tables. Then the coal chunks were put through a jig, or a shaker screen, to sort them according to size."

Together, they moved into the tunnel. Jolene shivered. It was cold underground. Cold and damp.

"In the Crowsnest Pass," said Karen, "the coal seams aren't horizontal like they are in many other mines. They run on pitches or inclines. This mine had a thirty-five degree pitch while the Frank mine was almost eighty degrees. The miners first had to build the gangway and then mine upwards on the incline." Karen scratched the back of her left hand, leaned against the rough wooden timbers supporting the tunnel and indicated an opening that extended upwards on the right-hand side.

"This is a room where the miners extracted the coal," explained Karen. "There are rooms like this one going all the way to the surface on different levels."

Jolene swung her headlamp towards the opening, the light sweeping across the open space of the room. A small wooden chute lined with metal protruded from one side. Black chunks of coal glistened at its bottom.

"The miners left huge blocks of coal called pillars to support the roof in between the rooms. Then they dug tunnels called raises upwards towards the surface. The raises were intersected by crosscut tunnels so that the whole thing looked like a three-dimensional checkered game board."

"What a job," observed Dad.

Karen picked up a metal pick that was leaning against the wall of the tunnel and handed it to Dad. "When the miners came to a coal face, they used a pick like this one to make a trench at the bottom of it. The trench was about as high as the pick and extended three metres back into the coal face."

"Then, they took a breast auger like that one," she said, indicating a metre-long auger beside Grandpa, "and drilled shot holes in the coal face above the trench for the charges." Grandpa spiralled the hand drill through the air.

"When the charges exploded, the coal collapsed into the

trench instead of shooting upwards or out into the room. Then the chunks were shovelled down a chute like this one into a waiting coal car." Karen indicated the wooden chute Jolene had noticed earlier.

Jolene could almost hear the scraping of shovels and tapping of picks. She looked up into the room, her hardhat and headlamp slipping backwards. Dad caught them with one hand. "Some miner you'd make," he teased. "You'd lose your light in a second."

"Actually," said Karen, "the earliest miners here didn't wear headlamps like we have. They wore canvas caps with Alladin lamps. Those were oil lamps that had open flames."

"Oil lamps with open flames," repeated Dad, taking notes. "Wasn't that dangerous?"

"It was," agreed Karen. "These mines were full of coal dust and methane gas. A spark from a pick or a falling rock could ignite the methane gas. Then the coal dust would explode like a bomb."

"So why did they have open flames in here?" asked Jolene.

"That's all the light they had back then," said Karen. "There weren't any electric lamps like ours." Her pager beeped and she stopped to answer it. "It's the town office. We should call them before they break for lunch. There's a phone in the orientation centre at the entrance."

"Okay," agreed Dad. "I'll come with you."

After they had gone, Jolene touched the glistening walls.

"It must have been awful working underground," she told Grandpa. But Grandpa did not respond. She looked around for him.

He was a few metres ahead, peering up into the room. She joined him, bobbing her hardhat to throw the light into the opening. "What are you looking at?" she asked, seeing nothing except dust speckling the beam of her lamp. Grandpa's light shone in her eyes and she squinted.

"Come and see," he said slowly. He put an arm around her shoulder, pulled her towards him and pointed one finger into the darkness. "Can you see them?"

A hot breeze brushed past Jolene as if someone had just opened a window on a summer day. Ahead of her, beams of light bobbed up and down in a large open space surrounded by walls of coal. She closed her eyes and then opened them again. Two men swung picks into the bottom of the coal face.

"Who are those guys?" she whispered.

"Miners, in this mine, in the early 1900s." Grandpa grinned at her.

"Miners? In the early 1900s?"

Grandpa nodded and pointed. "They're getting ready to blast."

Jolene squinted into the darkness, then turned back to stare at Grandpa, her green eyes wide in amazement. "You mean . . . " she began, but the voice of a miner interrupted her and she watched, mesmerized.

"That ought to do it eh, Gus?" asked the younger one. He leaned wearily on his pick, removed his cap and smoothed back his matted, blond hair.

The older miner peered into the space they had made with their picks, and then spoke to his young apprentice. "Afraid not, Steve." He swung his pick again.

"Ah, come on, Gus, it just has to be enough so the coal can move a little."

"That it does." Gus continued to pick at the coal face.

Grandpa snickered. "Steve, the young guy, he's a greenhorn."

"A greenhorn?" echoed Jolene.

"A brand new miner, and young, too. The fire boss must have paired these two up."

Jolene watched as the two men continued to pick a trench in the base of the coal face. Finally, Gus laid his pick at his feet. He inspected the crevice they had made. "That should do it," Gus said quietly. "Have you got the auger?"

Steve reached into the darkness and Jolene heard the clank of metal. He held up a heavy breast auger like the one Grandpa had picked up earlier.

"We'll need about a dozen shot holes, I reckon," said Gus.

Steve cranked steadily and the spiralling metal bit disappeared into the coal face, time after time. After each shot hole was drilled, Steve withdrew the auger and let it drop, bracing himself for a moment, sweat dripping from his forehead. Finally, after the last hole was drilled, he let the heavy auger fall to the ground with a clatter.

"I'll clean the holes out and get the charges ready," offered Gus. "Sit yourself down and have a drink of water."

Steve nodded and disappeared into the thin shadows of his lamp. Jolene heard the tinny sound of a water can. She watched as Gus picked up a long metal rod and inserted it into each of the narrow, metre-deep holes that Steve had just drilled. "What's he doing now?"

"He has to clean the coal dust out of the hole before he can blast," explained Grandpa.

"Shouldn't we get out of here?"

Grandpa laughed. "We're not really in here," he explained. "We're only looking through a window."

Jolene's mind raced. She watched Gus reach down into the darkness and bring up a narrow cylinder with a long string attached to it. "Is that dynamite?"

"No, it's a coal powder charge. Watch. He'll put the charges into those holes he just drilled, run the fuses around a corner somewhere and wait for the fire boss."

Gus did just that, inserting charges into each shot hole, then winding the fuses together. Finally, taking the length of fuse with him, he walked backwards around a corner until the dim glow of his lamp had been completely absorbed. The blackness in the empty room was thick, deep and endless.

Jolene shivered. "What are they waiting for?"

"The fire boss," explained Grandpa. "He's the only one who can detonate the charge."

Footsteps shuffled through the tunnel and the fire boss

emerged. He studied the coal face, and then swept his light past the charges, down the length of the fuse and around the corner. Soon, he and his light had disappeared completely. Jolene held her breath. A roar ripped through the tunnel and the coal face exploded in a flash of light. Chunks of coal flew in all directions. She raised her arms to shield herself, but nothing touched her. Beside her, she heard Grandpa's soft laughter and she opened her eyes.

A heavy dust filtered through the miners' lights as they returned to the room. With picks and shovels, they began to loosen the coal, pulling it towards one side of the room. Jolene could hear the sound of coal falling somewhere in the distance.

"There's a chute over there. They'll shovel it down into a coal car like the one that Karen showed us. Then the horses will pull it to the tipple."

Gus struggled towards them, stepping through the loose coal and dust, and crawled upwards. Chunks of coal dislodged and fell on him. He ducked and braced himself, then continued to climb.

"Where's he going?" asked Jolene.

"Up, to do it all again."

"You mean, blast again?"

Grandpa nodded. "After . . ." His voice stopped abruptly. Steve, the young miner, had stopped shovelling and was leaning, exhausted, against the wall. His hands moved across his shirt pockets. "Oh, don't do that," breathed Grandpa.

"Don't do what?" Jolene watched the young man pull a cigarette case from his pocket.

"Light that cigarette. That would be awfully foolish."

"Smoking's stupid!" agreed Jolene, turning away from the window.

"Even more stupid in a coal mine, Jo. You heard what Karen said about the methane gas."

Jolene whirled back to the window, thoughts exploding inside her head. "Do something," she said sharply as the young miner dug out a box of matches.

"Can't," said Grandpa simply. "We can't, Jo."

"But if there's an explosion, he'll be killed."

"He and probably his partner, and maybe even some of the others below him."

"Don't just stand there," Jolene pleaded as the miner squeezed a match between his fingers. "Do something!"

"Do something about what?" asked Dad's voice behind her.

Jolene spun around to face Dad and then turned back towards the miners, but the window had closed. Ahead of her stretched the old room that Karen had shown them. The miners had been absorbed by the glistening blackness. She stared hard at her grandfather, a million questions racing through her head as Karen rejoined them. Was she losing her mind, too?

Karen indicated a wooden board complete with numbers, hooks, and tags, on the wall of the main tunnel. "As the miners filled the cars, the drivers tagged them with metal tags like this one," said Karen, displaying a round tag. "These showed who had mined the coal the car held."

Grandpa explained. "The miners were paid by the amount of coal delivered to the mine entrance. The more coal they took out of the mine, the more money they made."

"How much did they make?" asked Dad.

"About twenty-two dollars a week," said Karen.

"Which was good money for those days," Grandpa added.

Jolene followed Karen farther into the dark tunnel, glancing back at the opening of the room behind them. Maybe the whole thing had been her imagination. Or maybe Grandpa wasn't as crazy as he'd sounded last night.

"Mining was dangerous work," said Karen. "Many men were injured by falling coal. Sometimes the fans went down or the air vents got blocked. Without air from outside circulating inside the mine, the concentration of methane gas would rise and that meant trouble."

"How many explosions were there in this mine?" asked Dad.

"A few," said Karen, "but in the worst one here in the Bellevue mine, thirty miners and one rescuer were killed."

Jolene shivered, remembering Steve's fingers pressed to strike the match. "What caused it?"

"No one really knows," said Karen. "The level of methane gas had been high for a few weeks though and the men had been worried. It could have been started by a spark from a falling rock or a pick."

"Or from a match being lit?" asked Jolene.

"I suppose. Most of the men knew better, but there were always a few."

Jolene stood in silence trying to imagine an underground explosion.

"If there was an explosion or an accident, the mine manager would sound three long whistles. That meant there was trouble in the mine."

"Trouble in the mine?" Jolene was surprised at how high and scared her voice was. They walked onwards in the thick silence.

"Before we go back out," said Karen, "I'm going to ask you all to switch off your headlamps. Then, I'll switch off mine."

One by one, Dad, Grandpa and Jolene switched off their lamps. Only a small halo of light shimmered against Karen's jacket until it was also extinguished. Immediately the darkness smothered Jolene. She turned her head one way and then the other searching for Grandpa or Dad or Karen, but couldn't make out any of them. The darkness closed in on her. It stole her air.

"If you close your eyes and then open them, you'll find that there's no real difference," said Karen's voice. Jolene closed her eyes. She opened them. The same thick blackness pressed in on her. She raised her hand in front of her face, but her fingers brushed her nose before she was able to see them. Jolene inhaled the darkness, a darkness as black as a raven, as deep as the earth.

"After three to five minutes in total darkness, it's almost impossible to tell which way is up and which way is down."

Karen's words swirled around Jolene's ears. She heard her own heartbeat echo through the tunnel and reached sideways, brushing Dad's jacket. Dad switched on his headlamp and instantly, a beam of light freed them from the darkness. One by one, Jolene, Grandpa and Karen did the same. Karen led them back towards the entrance.

Jolene turned slowly around as the light from outside infiltrated the mine. "It must have been awfully dark and dirty."

"Very dirty!" agreed Karen. "Later on, they built the washhouse. The original one still stands at the top of the hill." She laughed. "I'm sure the men appreciated it, but not half as much as their wives."

"Did any women work in the mines?" asked Jolene.

"Never underground. It was considered bad luck for a woman to be underground." Karen walked the final steps down the gangway. "Mining was tough work even for a strong man. But coal was the main fuel source back then. It heated the homes, ran the steam trains and fueled the smelters. They used to call it 'black gold.'"

"Do you come from a mining family, Karen?" asked Dad.

"I don't remember my family," said Karen softly, a distant

look creeping into her eyes. "I was separated from them when I was quite young."

They reached the mine entrance and stepped out into the sunshine. Jolene felt its soft embrace. She turned and stared at the tunnel behind her, imagining what it must have been like to be swallowed by the mountain day after day.

Chapter Four

Jolene woke to the flash of a bright light and the boom of an explosion. Coal hurtled in all directions, but when she opened her eyes, only the yellow of her bedroom walls greeted her. All night long, she had dreamed of Gus and Steve and held her breath while Steve pressed the match between his fingers. Had any of it been real? Was Grandpa such a good storyteller that he could make her imagination follow his? She heard the click of the front door closing. Dad, she knew, was off for a meeting and that would finally give her an opportunity to talk to Grandpa about what had happened in the mine yesterday. Dad had hovered about them all evening and Grandpa had gone to bed early last night. But now she wanted an explanation.

The house was empty. A note on the table read *Karen's*

taking us to the interpretive centre this afternoon. Underneath it, Grandpa had scrawled, Gone for a walk. Jolene frowned. She dressed hurriedly, grabbed a pen and added, Gone with Gramps to the note.

The air was ripe with summer. Jolene ran across to the crest of the hill and surveyed the valley, where the slide fanned out like an enormous grey hand. Below her, she spotted Grandpa crossing the highway. She scurried down the hillside and trailed him, ducking behind aspen trees to stay hidden. Grandpa crossed the railway tracks and turned onto a dirt road. She hurried to close the gap between them. The road passed a tired rodeo grounds, two grey horses and a freshly painted barn, before it curved into the slide.

Grandpa paused a few metres into the slide and Jolene scampered behind a large, nearby boulder covered in moss and lichens. Burrs, like tiny hedgehogs, clung to her socks and boots. Between the rocks, young trees reached for the sun. Grandpa surveyed the chunks of mountain around him. Then he came towards the large boulder that hid Jolene. She shrunk behind the rock and watched as he stepped into a dark shadow beside her. There, he stopped, closed his eyes as if in deep thought, and braced himself in anticipation.

Anxiety filled her. "Hey!" she cried, jumping forward. She reached out to grab Grandpa's arm and was instantly absorbed into the hot, tangible shadow. Sweat beaded her face and throat and she felt feverish. The shadows grew deeper, darker and denser. Her skin felt tight as if it were being stretched like an elastic band. She strained against the pressure, unable to clench her fingers into a fist, unable to close her eyes, unable to breathe. Suddenly, a great rush of hot air knocked her off balance. She was sucked forward and the darkness was gone. She stood trembling in the light, her breath coming in frantic gasps and her head spinning.

Where was she? What had happened? Fear squeezed her from the inside out. And where was Grandpa? Jolene's body shook. She looked up and a warm wind caressed her face. Ahead of her stretched a spring valley in the shadow of a mountain. Fuzzy crocuses grew at her feet and from somewhere close by came the rush of water. Beside her was an erratic, a large, solitary boulder left behind by a glacier. She heard a man's laugh and whirled around. A few steps away, grinning at her and playing with his moustache, stood Grandpa. "Gramps!" She ran to him and clutched his hands. "What happened? Where are we? How did we get here?"

"You're a natural," he chuckled. "Either that or I pulled you through the time crease with me."

"A natural what?" asked Jolene.

"Crazy person," laughed Grandpa. He gestured towards the mountain. "Welcome to the old town of Frank."

Jolene glanced at Turtle Mountain, its face intact. Gone was the fan of boulders that she had seen from the crest of the hill. "Before the slide?"

Grandpa nodded. "1903, if I had to guess."

Jolene released his hands and turned around slowly, taking it all in. So she hadn't imagined it in the mine yesterday. Grandpa hadn't been pretending after all. He really had found a way to go back in time and he wasn't senile either, at least not if any of this was real. She reached down and touched a wild rose bush. "Ouch!" The thorns were definitely real. Somewhere not far away, a train whistle sounded. She gazed up at the mountain again. "How did we get here?"

"We came through a time crease," Grandpa said simply. "I figured you could do it. It runs in the family."

Jolene was still turning, taking it all in. "You said something about that yesterday. Tell me again."

"Think of it this way," explained Grandpa. "Time is continuous, kind of like a long, long ribbon. So one moment never really ends and another never really begins. Any specific instant on the continuum has the properties of the continuum itself. That means that the past, present and future are not really separate times — they're all one."

Jolene nodded slowly, trying to picture a ribbon of time.

"But energy isn't continuous. And sometimes when there's lots of energy in a place, it gets trapped in this time continuum. Kind of like a crease in the ribbon. That's what those hot shadows are — time creases — places where the energy got trapped. Creases that you can slip through."

"So we just slipped through a time crease into 1903." It was partly a statement, partly a question. "And Aunt Peggy and her father could do this, too?"

Grandpa nodded.

"What happened to Dad? How come he isn't one of the lucky ones?"

"I'm not sure he'd want to be. Some would call it lucky. Others would call it crazy."

Others, like Mom, already called it crazy. "Do you think Aunt Peggy was crazy?"

Grandpa shook his head. "No, I think that Peggy's father shared the secret with her. I only discovered how to go back into the past a few years ago after I found your great-great-grandfather's journal."

"And here we are in my great-great-grandfather's town. Didn't he live here in 1903?"

"He did, but not for long," replied Grandpa. "According to his journal, they were good days though."

Jolene grinned at Grandpa. "Are these the *good old days?*"

"Why don't you decide for yourself? Want to check out the town?"

"Okay," she agreed. "Which way?"

"First, we better do something about those clothes, don't you think?"

Jolene looked down at her denim shorts and striped shirt. "What's wrong with them?"

"You would hardly be inconspicuous in 1903 dressed like that."

"Or you," said Jolene pointing at Grandpa's shiny baseball jacket.

"Come on then. I've got an idea." Jolene followed Grandpa, jumping across the muddy spots in the field. Ahead, in the shadow of the mountain, a ranch house stood not far from the river.

Cautiously, Grandpa made his way to the back of the house. Freshly laundered sheets billowed on the clothesline. Grandpa pointed to a long, grey skirt, stockings, bloomers and a puffy white long-sleeved blouse. "Those should fit you."

"Yuck!" said Jolene, crinkling up her nose. "Girls don't really wear that stuff, do they?"

Grandpa laughed. He removed his baseball jacket, pulled a cloth hat and a woolen jacket from the clothesline and put them on. The sleeves were a bit long, but otherwise he looked good. He pointed down the line where more clothes danced in the wind. "You could always be a boy," he suggested. "Didn't you say you wanted to just the night before last?"

Jolene's mind cartwheeled at the suggestion. Here, in the past, she could be a boy. It was a wonderful thought.

"Of course, someone could discover your secret."

That was true. She hesitated. Then again, it was 1903, she didn't know a soul and she could always slip through a time crease back into the future. Her smile stretched between her dimples. "So what!" she said. This was her chance to be a boy, to be a risk-taker like Michael.

"All right then," said Grandpa deftly sidestepping along-

side the clothesline and pulling garments from the line.
"Duck into those trees and change." Jolene did as she was
told, hiding herself in the trees and dressing quickly in
knee-length trousers, long socks, a long-sleeved shirt, a
short jacket and a cloth cap. At least she'd worn her hiking
boots. She handed Grandpa her shirt and shorts. He rolled
them up inside his jacket and hid them in the trees. "We'll
return our borrowed clothes on the way back," he explained,
joining her again.

"Do I look like a boy?"

"Close enough. Good thing you wear your hair short."

Jolene pulled her cap farther down on her head. For the
first time in her life she was glad of her boyish figure. Now
if she could just walk like a boy and talk like a boy and think
like a boy, maybe she could convince people that she was a
boy.

She swaggered through the grass with her head held
high. "How's this look?" she asked, lowering her voice.

Grandpa laughed at her. "Ridiculous."

She tried snappy, quick steps. "Any better?" she asked,
drawing out the syllables of the words.

"Sorry!"

Jolene threw up her hands. "Never mind then," she said
in her usual voice, falling into her regular stride.

"Now that's good!" said Grandpa.

They crossed the field and climbed up onto the railway
track. Jolene leapt along the railway ties, smooth enough to

dance barefoot on. In the distance, a gruff voice called and a whip snapped. "What's going on?" asked Jolene.

"Looks like they're building another railway line to the mine." The gruff voice barked again and Jolene watched a workhorse snort and labour to pull its heavy load up onto the railroad grade. Saws rasped beneath the smoky smell of green wood. The air echoed with the ring of hammers and the scrape of shovels.

"I bet those guys would appreciate a chainsaw," said Jolene.

"Careful what you say here," advised Grandpa. "Someone might think you're crazy."

They followed the tracks and soon reached a collection of canvas tents. "Must be the construction camp for the railway," said Grandpa. The aroma of bacon reached Jolene. A burly, red-bearded man pushed back the canvas flap of one of the tents and stepped outside. "Bet you he's the cook," said Grandpa.

A covered chuckwagon, its wheels listing, rested alongside the cook's tent. Large wooden barrels littered the camp, as did bits and pieces of bones and wood. "What a charming place in history," Jolene said sarcastically. "Where is everybody?"

"The men will all be out working now. They'll be back for supper."

Jolene's stomach growled as they crossed over onto a dirt road and she wished she'd had time for breakfast. A shiny object on the ground caught her eye. She stooped and dug a coin out of the mud.

"Two bits," said Grandpa as Jolene studied the 1903 coin. "That'll buy a whole lot more here than a quarter would at home." Jolene tucked the coin into her pocket.

On their left, a few small, wooden buildings stood, alone in their togetherness. From their midst, a horse whinnied. Then suddenly it reared, its black mane tossing and its hooves striking out in the air. "Wonder what's got into her?" asked Grandpa, turning towards the corral.

The animal whinnied and reared, whinnied and reared. A young man holding a muddy horse came out of the stable. Slowly, Grandpa approached the corral. Jolene followed tentatively. Grandpa extended a hand towards the frightened horse, clicking his tongue and speaking in a soothing tone. The horse stopped rearing. It pawed at the ground and then stood still. Grandpa reached out a hand to rub her velvety muzzle.

"Thanks," said the young man leading the other horse into the corral. "By the way, I'm Karl Johnson."

"Victor Basso," replied Grandpa, using a made-up last name. "And this is Jo."

"Your grandson, I expect," said Karl smiling. "Looks just like you — same eyes."

Jolene smiled proudly at her successful masquerade.

Karl pointed to the horse Grandpa was stroking. "That one there, Dusty, she's got a mind of her own. No telling what she's going to do some days." Jolene watched the eyes and ears of the horse. "Just wish they were all as predictable as Old Charlie here." Karl indicated the muddy draft horse behind him.

"Well, there's predictable and then there's predictable." Grandpa's eyes glimmered. Jolene recognized the look of a story. "I remember when I was working in the mines up north," he began. "There was one horse in particular, Jake his name was, Genius Jake."

"Genius Jake?" echoed Karl.

"Jake, the genius horse." The words squeezed through the bristles of Grandpa's moustache. "He was what you'd call predictable."

"But how did he get his name?" asked Jolene. Already, the possible answers swirled in her mind.

"Genius Jake was the only horse I ever knew that could count and tell time."

Karl guffawed and Dusty skittered. Grandpa reached out a steadying hand to the horse and Jolene clambered up onto the railing of the corral.

"Mining horses come and go," began Grandpa, "like miners. Some can't bear the dark, some the coal colours their lungs, some move on to other things. But not Jake. Jake had pulled coal cars in the mine for as long as anyone could remember. Always seven, seven coal cars, and no more than seven."

Jolene watched Grandpa's eyes come alive. "Once the

coal cars are full, they're hitched together with steel con- necting pins," Grandpa told Jolene. "Old Jake, he'd listen for those seven chinks of sound, and then, as soon as the last one was hitched, away he'd go down that tunnel. Never had to ask him, bribe him or whip him. He just went and the men, they respected old Jake for that. He was as reliable and predictable a horse as ever there was."

Reliable and predictable. They were, Jolene decided, words that described her. Or rather, they were words that had once described her.

Karl's voice intruded on her thoughts. "Old Charlie here is pretty predictable, but I don't know if he can count."

"Jake could. And he did, every day. Every day the same thing. As predictable as summer after spring. Until one day, one day in particular. Only it wasn't Jake's fault. It was young Tony's fault and he should have known better."

Jolene waited expectantly. Old Charlie had turned to watch Grandpa. "Tony tried to trick that old horse, you see. He had eight coal cars to take out and he didn't want to make an extra trip back into the mine. So he wrapped the last connecting pin in his handkerchief and slid it into the link, quiet as a dandelion puff on the wind. Figured Jake wouldn't hear him."

Karl was following Grandpa's eyes. Even Dusty was lis- tening attentively, her ears perked. "And Jake didn't! Didn't hear the eighth car hook on, and he started off straining and snorting under that heavy load. Walked about half a dozen steps and then jolted to a standstill. Looked back over his shoulder and whinnied, loud and long. Knew right then, knew with the weight of the load that he'd been tricked, and he meant to let Tony know he knew. Opened his mouth and brayed like an angry donkey."

Grandpa brayed loudly. Dusty skittered again and Jolene almost fell off the railing. "Well, that braying ricocheted back and forth between the walls of the mine until it nearly drove Tony crazy, and the other men too. But Jake refused to stop, wouldn't budge, wouldn't pull, wouldn't even shut his mouth long enough to listen to Tony's apology. And then, all of a sudden, he stopped, just fell silent. And before Tony could say a word, the mine whistle blew. It was quitting time. See, Jake had worked in the mines so long that he knew when it was time to quit, knew before the whistle even blew, knew without being told that there was no point complaining any more that day. The way I see it, he was a genius horse that could count and tell time."

Karl laughed and Old Charlie blustered, showing his teeth. Jolene savoured the story of Genius Jake and wondered how much truth there was in it.

Karl rubbed Old Charlie's muzzle. "I'd best get this one brushed," he said, extending a hand to Grandpa. "Thank you for the help and the tale."

"Pleasure's been mine," said Grandpa, and Jolene knew it had been. She jumped down from the fence, lost her balance and fell into a pile of dry horse manure. Grandpa dug a handkerchief out of his pocket and handed it to her as they started down the road.

Karl called from the stable door. "By the way, I got myself a little room in the loft up above the stable. There's an empty one alongside mine if you need a place to stay for a few nights."

"I'll keep that in mind," said Grandpa. "Thank you."

Dusty whinnied and Karl called after them again. "There's a wooden bridge that crosses Gold Creek just up ahead. That'll take you past the cottages and directly into town to Dominion Avenue." He turned and disappeared into the stables.

Chapter Five

On the road into the town of Frank, Jolene tried to match Grandpa's stride. "Have you always told stories, Gramps?"

"Nope!" said Grandpa without hesitation. "Used to be scared stiff to talk in public."

"Really? You're such a natural. I just figured that you'd wanted to tell stories all your life."

"Oh, I did," said Grandpa. "As I kid, I loved to hear my mother and my uncles tell stories. I'd rehearse them in bed, trying out different phrases and different voices, night after night. But I could never bring myself to tell them to anybody else."

"Why?"

"What if they didn't like them? What if they didn't laugh

when they were supposed to?" He paused, remembering. "What if they laughed at me?"

"So how did you finally get over that?"

"I started going down to the stable every night to groom the horses. And after they were all brushed, I would stand there in front of them and tell them a bedtime story." Jolene laughed and Grandpa continued. "They'd just look at me with these big brown eyes and listen until I was finished. I remember thinking that horses were the best listeners around until I learned that they sleep with their eyes open." Jolene smiled fondly at Grandpa. "But after that, whenever I felt nervous about talking to a group of people, I'd just imagine they were all horses."

Jolene made a mental note to remember that as she followed Grandpa over a little wooden bridge and past a row of seven cottages. One of the doors opened and a tall, broad-shouldered man hustled out onto the road, whistling. To Jolene's surprise, Grandpa fell into step beside him. "Good day," said Grandpa. "I was wondering if I might find work here."

"Aye, I expect you will. The town's booming." The man stretched out a hand. "Warren MacEachern."

"Victor Basso." The two men shook hands.

Jolene studied Warren's hands — big, broad, rough hands, scrubbed palms with black creases — a coal miner's hands.

"I'm headed uptown if you'd like to come along. Some of the lads up there should be able to tell you more," suggested Warren.

"Pa, wait up!" A boy bolted from the door of the cottage and caught up with them.

"Did you cut that kindling for yer Ma?" asked his father sternly.

"Aye, and brought up the coal as well."

"All right then, Daniel. This is Mr. Basso and . . . "

"My grandson, Jo," added Grandpa. Daniel nodded in Jolene's direction. She pulled her cap down farther over her eyes. The boy was a little taller than herself, lean and angular, and probably about her age, she guessed. Freckles splattered his face beneath straight auburn hair. He was dressed much like she was, minus the cap.

Ahead of them stretched the town of Frank in 1903 — long before she'd been born. Jolene chuckled to herself and kept pace with Daniel. In town, she stopped and looked sideways, down a broad dirt road lined with buildings and wooden sidewalks. It must be Dominion Avenue. But Warren turned left instead, angling towards the base of Turtle Mountain.

"I'm off to a baseball practice at the rec field," said Warren.

"Really?" remarked Grandpa. "I used to play a little baseball."

That, Jolene knew, was an understatement. Dad had told her that if he'd had enough money, Grandpa could have played in the major leagues. Even at the age of seventy-two he played well.

"Well, you're welcome to come along if you like. We've

got a pretty good team, but unfortunately one of our big hitters is out injured. He climbed into one of the big chutes to dislodge some coal and fell in — almost got crushed by the falling coal." In her mind, Jolene could see Gus shield himself against the bouncing chunks of coal.

"How is working in the mine here?" asked Grandpa.

"Pretty fair, I guess. The seams are soft and the coal around here is clean. You've mined before?"

Grandpa nodded as a large field came into view at the base of the mountain. "It's early in the season," said Warren as they approached the other men. "But the weather's been fair, so we thought we ought to have a few practices before we play."

The two men left to join the other ball players and Daniel pointed ahead to a stand of nearby trees. "Race you," he cried. Jolene sprinted after him, but he'd had a head start and was already shinnying up the trunk of the biggest tree by the time she caught up with him. Grabbing the first handhold, she started to climb. She slipped once, her boot scraping the bark, then finally finding a foothold.

"You climb like a girl," said Daniel scornfully, watching her pull herself up beside him.

Jolene scowled at him. She hadn't thought about trying to climb trees like a boy. Besides, Michael climbed them the same way she did when he climbed, which wasn't often. He was scared of heights.

"Look out for that eagle!" Daniel pointed up in the air.

Jolene's hands went up to protect her face and she lost her balance. She caught herself upside down on the branch. Beside her, Daniel roared with laughter. Jolene pulled herself upright and gave him a dirty look.

Voices called as the men began batting practice. "Your grandpa's up," said Daniel. "Isn't he a bit old to play?" The pitcher wound up and then uncoiled. Grandpa let the first one go by and circled the bat in the air.

"Bet he can't hit Frank MacKenzie's ball," Daniel said smugly. He dug a wooden whistle out of his pocket and began to play.

Jolene admired the smooth, polished wood of the whistle. "Where'd you get that?"

"Made it myself." Daniel blew into it and a shrill trill filled the air.

"I'll bet you two bits against that whistle that my grandpa hits it out of the park," challenged Jolene as Grandpa let another ball go by.

"Two bits!" exclaimed Daniel. "Let's see."

Jolene dug into her pocket and produced the coin she'd found earlier.

"You're on!" The bat cracked and the ball sailed over the far edge of the field. A cry went up from the men. "Wow!" breathed Daniel.

Jolene held out her hand for the whistle. Daniel glowered at her, then turned it over reluctantly. She stuffed it into her pocket. That would teach him to be arrogant. She glanced up at the snow-capped mountain in front of her. Suddenly, she didn't want to watch the baseball practice. She wanted to do something brave, something different. "Have you ever climbed Turtle Mountain?" she asked Daniel.

"Just to the lookout to see the town."

It wasn't quite like climbing the mountain, but at least it was a start. "Can we go?"

Daniel studied her for a moment. "Sure," he said jumping down from the branch. Jolene did the same. They skirted the ball field and ducked down a dirt trail leading into the surrounding forest. Branches hung low over the path, filtering the sunlight.

"This here's a bear trail," said Daniel as the forest enveloped them.

"Really?" Jolene slowed. She'd never done much hiking, but she'd heard lots of stories about bears.

"It's about the right time of the year for bears now. They're hungry in the spring, too." Jolene stopped walking. Daniel also stopped and motioned for her to pass him. "You can go first if you like. Bears usually attack from behind."

Jolene edged past him into the deepening shadows of the pine trees. Fear prickled her. "You know, I never told my grandfather where I was going. Maybe I should go back before he starts looking for me."

Daniel scraped the sap off a tree trunk. "Scared?" he taunted.

"No!" lied Jolene. "I just don't want Gramps to worry."

"We'll be able to see the field from the lookout — if you want to go on, that is," challenged Daniel.

Jolene started up the path again with Daniel close behind. "Besides," said Daniel, "there's mostly black bears around here. They're not so fierce as grizzlies. Usually they just maul you." There was a long pause. "Happened last year. Two young miners hiking up Turtle Mountain when they came upon this big male black bear feeding on berries."

"Were they killed?"

"Nope," said Daniel. "One of them lost his right elbow. The other had his lower jaw torn off."

Jolene's stomach flopped at the thought of a jawless face. "How much farther?" she asked to take her mind off things.

"Not much," said Daniel. Jolene resumed her route, her eyes scanning the forest. The skin on the back of her neck felt cold and clammy. Snap! She whirled around to face Daniel. "What was that?"

"What was what?"

Jolene walked on. Snap! Crack! "That!" Jolene froze in her tracks, listening.

"I didn't hear nothing."

"It sounded like branches breaking, like a big animal moving through the trees." She wiped her forehead with the heel of her palm. "I think we should go back."

Daniel stared into her face. "Now you even sound like a girl," he said disgustedly.

Jolene stared defiantly back at him as he pointed at a short, rocky cliff above them. "The lookout's right there."

For a moment, Jolene hesitated. What if they ran into a bear, a hungry bear just emerging from hibernation? Her skin tingled with danger, but she made a conscious attempt to dismiss it. She had elected to disguise herself as a boy because boys were risk-takers. Here was her chance to be one. She took a deep breath and started up towards the lookout. Suddenly, the branches beside her shook and a furry animal dashed in front of her. "Aah!" screamed Jolene, jumping back into Daniel, her legs trembling and her heart thumping.

"Run, it's a man-eating rodent!" screamed Daniel, pointing at a furry red squirrel that sat in a nearby branch chattering. He doubled over laughing.

Jolene narrowed her eyes at him and gritted her teeth. Then she turned and ran ahead. He didn't have to be such a jerk and she intended to tell him so. "Look," she said, stopping and turning back to face Daniel without warning.

The branch in Daniel's hand snapped in two. He stood holding the broken wood as the significance of the scene registered in Jolene's mind.

"You!" she exclaimed, grabbing one piece of the dry wood and snapping it in half. "You were making those noises all along."

Daniel leaned against a tree and laughed. He held his stomach and laughed and laughed.

Jolene hurled the branch down and raced the rest of the way up to the base of the lookout. What a fool she was! How could she be so gullible?

"You should have seen your face," teased Daniel catching up with her. "You looked like a scared little girl."

Jolene scrambled away from him, up the side of the rocky lookout. She took a deep breath, exhaled and surveyed the valley. Below her stretched the town of Frank. She could see Dominion Avenue, the mine entrance and the ball field where Grandpa and the other men were still practising. She did not look back as Daniel scrambled up behind her. Instead, she plunked herself down on the edge of the rocky cliff, dug out Daniel's whistle and started to play.

"Your face looked . . . "

Jolene blew loud enough to drown out his words, to drown out his presence in her mind.

Halfway through a simple tune, Jolene felt a hand on her shoulder. Daniel stood with his back to her and to the edge of the cliff. She shrugged him off and polished the whistle on her trousers.

Daniel's voice was barely a whisper. "Jo, there's, there's a bear."

"Right!" She blasted a shrill bleat on the wooden whistle.

Daniel's fingers gripped her shoulder. "Look."

Jolene blew three quick notes. "Don't worry," she said without turning around. "It will probably go for me first."

"Jo, please!" Daniel's voice was panicky.

But she would not be so easily fooled this time. "Besides," she continued, "if it's a black bear, it will only maul you or tear off a limb or two." She blasted a long note. "Then again," she added thoughtfully, "it is spring and bears are hungry at this time of year."

Beside her, Daniel's feet backed towards the edge of the cliff. Jolene heard a curious huffing. "That's very good," she told Daniel. "You do a good bear impersonation."

Daniel made no response. Jolene played a short tune on the whistle. It was a bit like the recorder that she played in school. "This is a good whistle," she said looking up at Daniel for the first time since she had run up the lookout. His face was a ghostly white and his eyes, resembling dark moons, were fixed directly in front of him. Slowly, Jolene turned her head and followed Daniel's gaze.

A black bear stood sniffing the air at the edge of the bushes behind them, about twenty metres away. It swung its head back and forth. "A b-b-bear," she stammered, rising to her feet and crowding close to Daniel.

The animal stared intently at Jolene. Then suddenly it charged at them. Jolene grasped Daniel's arm as they teetered on the edge of the rocky cliff. Just a few metres from them, the bear veered to the right into the bushes, slapping its front foot against a tree trunk and huffing violently.

Jolene trembled. "What's it doing?" she whispered.

The bear opened and closed its mouth in rapid succession making a loud popping noise. It bared its teeth at them.

"I don't know, but we've got to get out of here," said Daniel. Clutching Jolene's arm, he took a small step sideways.

Immediately, the bear charged a second time, this time stopping directly in front of them. It turned its head, averted its eyes and panted.

"Don't move," whispered Jolene, forcing her body to stop shaking. She and Daniel stood like statues. The bear reared slightly, then turned and lumbered away. At the edge of the trees, it paused and looked back over its shoulder. Jolene held her breath and closed her eyes. Would it charge again? This time for real? She heard a deep gurgling growl and waited.

"It's gone." Daniel's voice floated into her ear.

She opened her eyes. The bear had disappeared. The sun shone high above Turtle Mountain. "I thought you were just tricking me," she said as the energy flooded out of her body.

Daniel's face was covered in beads of sweat. His hands shook. "We better go," he advised. "Before it comes back."

Jolene needed no further urging. Together, they sprinted down the forest path and burst out onto the baseball field just as the men were packing up. Jolene started to run towards Grandpa, but Daniel's hand caught her arm. "Jo,

I'm sorry about the trickery and the girl comments," he said sheepishly. "Ain't no way no girl could have stayed so calm up there with that bear charging at us."

Jolene put a hand to her mouth to cover her smile. Daniel's eyes pleaded with her. "But, please don't say anything to your grandpa or my pa about the bear. If Pa finds out, well, I'll be in a heap of trouble."

Jolene did not respond immediately. It would serve him right if he got into a heap of trouble. But, if Grandpa found out that she'd had an encounter with a bear, well, he might not be so pleased either. "I won't say anything if you won't," she promised.

Daniel beamed at her. "Come on," he said. "I'll race you." They sprinted to the baseball field, arriving at virtually the same instant.

"Will you join us for a drink, Victor?" asked one of the men.

Grandpa looked across at Jolene. "Another time. Best look after the young one here."

"Well thanks for comin' out," said Warren, shaking Grandpa's hand. "We'll see you back then?"

"I hope so." Grandpa stole a glance at Jolene. She hoped so too.

She waved goodbye to Daniel. "We best hurry," said Grandpa as they turned onto the road. "We have to get back in time to go to the interpretive centre."

They walked in silence. She'd just travelled a century

through time, become a boy, had her first encounter with a bear and here she was walking along as if nothing unusual had happened.

"So are you feeling braver?" asked Grandpa.

Jolene chewed on a smile. She'd certainly shown courage back there on the lookout. "Yes," she said firmly, feeling her body fill with a sense of pride. "Yes, I am."

Grandpa smiled and said nothing.

They found their clothes and changed in the trees. "We didn't even get a chance to meet our ancestors," noted Jolene. "I think we should leave these clothes here for when we come back." Jolene rolled up the clothes she had borrowed.

Grandpa threw back his head and laughed. He stuffed their borrowed garments into a hollow tree trunk. "All right, but we have to return them eventually."

They set off in the direction of the erratic. "How do we get back anyway?" asked Jolene as the rush of the river reached her ears.

"It's all a matter of perspective. Once you find the crease where the energy's trapped, you change the way you think of yourself in time."

Jolene watched him, a bewildered look on her face.

Grandpa sighed. "Not being a physicist, I didn't understand everything in the journal. But your great-great-grandfather wrote about there being two ways to perceive motion, and I think it might be the same for the passage of time."

"Huh?"

"Let me show you." Grandpa walked through a grove of trees towards the crystal river and Jolene followed. He picked up a stick. "I think that there may be two ways to think of yourself in time. The usual way is to move with time as you would if you followed a stick floating downstream." He threw the stick into the river and they watched it drift away. Then he walked a few strides and pointed at a large rock in the river. "The other way is to fix yourself at one location and watch as time passes over you."

"So when you find a time crease, you situate yourself in that one place and let time change," paraphrased Jolene.

"That's my thought," said Grandpa, leading her across the field towards the erratic where they had first found themselves in 1903. "And the energy that's trapped there pulls or pushes you through time."

"Do you ever end up not going back to the present, going to another time?" asked Jolene.

"I haven't yet," said Grandpa. "Thank goodness." He pointed to the large solitary boulder left behind by the glacier. "There's the time crease there. See that deep shadow?" Grandpa reached down and took Jolene's hand. Together, they stepped into the dense shade. It felt warm and alive.

"Now think of yourself as stationary in time at this location," advised Grandpa. "And let the energy push you through the crease." He closed his eyes.

A warm breeze hit Jolene and once again her body was

stretched, caught in darkness between the past and the present. Then suddenly there was a blast of hot air and she lost her balance, falling forward into the light. One hand found the rough surface of a boulder and the other one touched the shiny material of Grandpa's jacket. "We're back," she gasped, looking around at Frank Slide and reorienting herself.

"Actually we're forward," said Grandpa, catching his breath, his hands on his knees. He straightened up. "Oh, you might not want to say too much about this to your father," he advised. "He might think we're both crazy."

Jolene walked thoughtfully beside Grandpa. Her body felt tired and worn, like Grandpa's steps. It was no wonder he looked exhausted some days and made some inappropriate comments from time to time. Now, for certain, she knew he wasn't senile, but how was she ever going to convince her mom and dad?

Chapter Six

"That's a picture of the town before the slide," said Karen, looking over Jolene's shoulder. They were standing in the Frank Slide Interpretive Centre and Jolene was studying the photos in front of her. She spotted the railway tracks, the ranch house where they had borrowed the clothes drying on a line, the railway construction camp and the road they had walked along. Beside it was the stable where Grandpa had told her, Karl, Dusty and Old Charlie his story. On the other side of Gold Creek were Daniel's home and the other cottages surrounding it.

"And," said Karen, gesturing sideways at another photo, "there's a picture of the town after the slide."

Jolene's eyes flickered from one photograph to the other and back again. Daniel's cottage, all the cottages were missing in the second one. "Is this the part that was buried?" she asked, outlining an area that included the cottages and the time crease.

Karen nodded. "As you can see, only a small part of the town was hit, including these miners' cottages, the stable, the shoe shop, some ranches, the railway construction camp and the mine itself." Karen indicated each building on the photo. "But, even some of those people directly in the path of the slide survived."

"They did?" Jolene looked out the window of the Frank Slide Interpretive Centre. Huge boulders tumbled through her mind and filled the valley below her. How could anyone have survived a slide like this? In her mind, she saw Karl holding Old Charlie and heard Daniel's footsteps on the road. "I thought it would have buried everything in its path."

"Scientists believe that a huge slab of rock near the top of the mountain broke off. It skidded down the mountain face, breaking into boulders, but not actually tumbling. When it reached the bottom of the valley, it scooped up mud from the river. It was that wall of rock and mud that hit the town and carried the houses forward, destroying some of them instead of burying them all." Karen paused. "Imagine that the slab of rock was a stacked deck of cards that you were holding and you threw them squarely onto a table. The deck would break apart into cards, but the individual cards would stay in the same order. And the top cards would stay on top and go the farthest."

"Some say the mine brought the mountain down." Grandpa's voice rose behind them.

"Mining did contribute to the slide, but it wasn't the main cause," replied Karen. "The way the mountain was formed millions of years ago is really why it slid. The upper part of Turtle Mountain is hard limestone. The base is softer, weaker rock — sandstone, shale and coal. Over the years, the river and glaciers washed away the rock at the bottom of the mountain, creating a ledge part way up. That made the mountain very unstable."

"So what did mining have to do with it then?" asked Jolene.

It was Grandpa that answered. "When you remove the guts of a mountain, it's bound to make it weaker."

Jolene tried to remember the face of Turtle Mountain as she had seen it that morning — a face protruding above a ledge, a face watching the town of Frank. "Dad said there was a big crack in it."

"There was and there still is," explained Karen. "The mountain slid at 4:10 on the morning of April 29, 1903. It had been hot for a few days and a lot of the snow in the mountains had melted. All the cracks filled up with water. Then, on the night of the slide, it got very cold again. The water in the cracks froze and expanded. Scientists think that might have triggered the slide."

Jolene's thoughts slipped beneath the rocks, imagining how it must have felt to be buried by a mountain.

"It took about ninety seconds for ninety million tons of rock to fall."

Grandpa let out a low whistle and Jolene did the mental calculations. That was a million tons of rock per second.

"The mass of limestone that slid was about 425 metres high, 900 metres wide and 150 metres thick. In some spots, it's 30 metres deep and the slide itself covers three square kilometres of the valley."

Jolene tried to envision that much rock screaming down the mountain face.

"That's a lot of rock," said Grandpa thoughtfully. "It must have made a terrific noise."

"Most people didn't even know what it was," said Karen. "Some thought it was an explosion in the mine. Others thought it was hail, an earthquake, even a volcano because there was so much dust."

Grandpa furrowed his brow. "How many people died?"

"About seventy in total," said Karen. "I can't believe that the men working the night shift in the mine weren't killed. It's a small miracle, really."

"The men in the mine weren't killed?"

"Well, three men at the mine entrance were. But the ones underground were safe, even though the entrance was buried by rock. It took them thirteen hours, but they managed to dig their way up through a coal seam to the surface." She smiled. "Only Old Charlie, the mine horse, had to stay behind, but there's an interesting story about him, too."

Jolene and Grandpa looked up at the same time.

"The company that owned the mine wanted it re-opened as soon as possible. About one month after the slide, they dug through the rubble to the main entrance. Out of the gangway staggered a very thin horse. Old Charlie had survived by drinking the water that had seeped through the rocks, eating the wood off the timbers in the mine and sucking his harness for salt."

Jolene sighed. At least Old Charlie had lived. She didn't want to think about the others.

Beside her, Grandpa smoothed his moustache. "Imagine that! Old Charlie made it."

"He did," Karen said. "Everyone rushed to give him a tremendous welcome. They fed him the finest oats and brandy, except it was too rich a diet for him and he died a few hours later."

"Guess he wasn't so predictable after all," said Jolene, raising her eyebrows at Grandpa.

Just then a voice announced that the audio-visual show was about to begin. "Let's catch the movie," Grandpa suggested, "then we can look at the displays."

Dad joined them at the theatre entrance. "Don't tell me that you're starting to take an interest in all these rocks and coal," he whispered to Jolene.

Jolene didn't respond. It was hardly the same when you could actually go back into the history of those rocks and coal, but she certainly couldn't tell Dad that.

After the show, Jolene wandered quickly through the displays, humming the theme song from the movie. Dad was busy making notes and reading newspaper clippings, paying careful attention to each and every detail.

Laughter rang out behind her and Jolene turned to see Grandpa and Karen pointing at something in one of the exhibits. Another story must have spilled out of Grandpa. Hopefully it hadn't been from an inappropriate time or place.

Jolene made her way through the gift shop and outside. Standing in the wind, she faced the shadows of the mountain, the shadows that her ancestors had once lived beneath, the shadows of disaster.

"Karen's taking me into the slide this afternoon," announced Dad the next day. "She's got a special permit to climb on the rocks. You're welcome to come along if you've changed your mind about rocks."

"Sure," said Jolene sheepishly.

"I think I'll pass," said Grandpa. "Climbing rocks is best left to young folks."

Jolene hesitated. "But we were planning to go to the dairy for an ice cream cone," she remembered. "Can we go later, Gramps?"

"You bet!"

It wouldn't take much to convince Grandpa to go for an ice cream, Jolene knew. Besides, climbing on the slide sounded like fun. "Stay close," she whispered to Grandpa as she followed Dad out the door. "At least in the past century."

They drove into the slide on the same road that she and

Grandpa had followed, except Karen took them much farther into the heart of the rocks. "It's beautiful country," said Dad. "Have you lived here all your life?"

"Actually, I have a rather mysterious past," said Karen. "When I was about twenty, I was found wandering in the hills near here, suffering from hypothermia and near starvation. I had amnesia and nobody recalls having seen me before or hearing anything about me. It was as if I had no past."

"Really!" Dad was amazed.

"So I don't know where I came from." Karen stopped the car. "But I think that I must have come from this area. It just feels like I did."

Jolene scrambled out of the car and up onto the rocks. In some ways, she had also come from this area. When her great-great-grandfather had come to Canada in 1903, he had brought his family to Frank. And she had visited that same town only yesterday. It was pretty amazing. In fact, the whole slide was amazing. She leaped from boulder to boulder. "Hey, this one looks like a huge brain and that one there looks like a pyramid."

Dad was balancing on a stone castle shooting a roll of film. "The mine entrance was just over there, on the south side of the river." He squatted down and angled the camera upwards at the scree part way up the mountain. Jolene jumped down from a large lichen-covered boulder and skirted some trees near the edge of the road. "I'd like to get as much of the mountain as possible in this shot," said Dad, backing up slightly.

"Watch out!" screamed Jolene as her father tumbled backwards off the edge of the boulder in a cartwheel of arms and legs. Jolene scrambled across the rocks until she reached the place where he had fallen. "Are you okay?"

"I think so," said Dad, pulling himself slowly to his feet. He rubbed his hipbone. "A little bruised maybe. Oh no!" He raised his camera to show Jolene the huge crack in the lens. "What do you think the chances are of finding one of these lenses here?"

The chances weren't good and after half an hour on the phone the next morning, Dad decided to head back to Calgary. "If I go today, I should be back by lunchtime tomorrow. You two want to come along?"

"I'd rather stay," said Grandpa.

Jolene looked sideways at her grandfather. She knew now that Grandpa would go back to the old town of Frank. Just three days ago, she would have jumped at the chance to go back to Calgary, to swim with Gerard. But now, maybe they could go back in time instead. Gerard would still be there when she got back. "I'd rather stay, too, if that's okay with Gramps."

Dad looked from Jolene to Grandpa and back to Jolene again with a look of surprise and delight. "All right, but promise you'll stick around here."

Grandpa chewed on a smile. "How far can we go? You've

got the car."

"How far without a car?" teased Jolene as they wandered along Bellevue's main street licking their ice cream cones.

"To the dairy, for a strawberry." Grandpa ran his tongue around the bumpy brim of his waffle cone.

"Down the street, on our feet."

"To the hill, when we've had our fill."

"To the mine, back in time," Jolene sang out mischievously.

Creamy blueberry ice cream ran down her fingers onto her wrist and dripped into sticky blue splotches at her feet. "Oh no!" she exclaimed, licking her fingers. The sun baked the ice cream on the sidewalk. "How far did you go yesterday?"

"1901. The official opening of the town of Frank. The coal company put on a big party. They brought in fresh fruit and ice cream." Grandpa held up his cone. "And a French chef, too. People came from all around, danced far into the night and tried their hands at the sporting events."

"That must have been quite the party. I wish I'd been there." Jolene bit the bottom of her cone and sucked the ice cream through it.

"You do, do you?"

She grinned at him, her lips a pale blue. "Are you sure that Dad can't go back through the creases?"

"He can't even see the windows," explained Grandpa. "Remember in the mine?"

Jolene recalled how the window had vanished when Dad had arrived. "Why not?"

"I don't exactly know. Maybe it has something to do with feeling and understanding the energy of history."

Jolene stopped walking. "But Dad likes history. He's a history fanatic. After all, he owns a museum."

"Of dead artifacts," added Grandpa. He sighed. "It's not the same, Jo."

"I know," she admitted, "but what can we do about it?"

Grandpa shrugged. "I wish I knew."

She wished she knew, too. And she wished that Dad could travel back in time. That would make it much easier to convince Dad that Grandpa wasn't crazy. Maybe if he went back and felt what it was like to live there, maybe he'd find a way to bring the museum alive. "Can we go back, please?" pleaded Jolene.

"Are you that anxious to be a boy again?"

Jolene hesitated. She did enjoy masquerading as a boy, but that wasn't the only reason she wanted to step back into 1903. "We have to go back." All night long, she had heard Daniel's voice, seen Karl's hand reach up and encircle Old Charlie's neck. "Those people we met — well, the stable and the cottages were buried by the slide. We have to warn them."

Grandpa touched two weathered fingers to Jolene's cheek. "There's no point, Jo."

"But Gramps, we can't just let them die."

Grandpa looked older than Jolene had ever seen him look. His tired eyes held hers. "There are some things you can't change," he said sadly. "Believe me, Jo, I know." He took a deep breath. "You never met my brother, George, who was killed in the war, but you remember Grandma. When I first discovered that I could go back, I thought that maybe I could make history take a different course. But it doesn't work. You can't change what happened in the past and it hurts too much to try."

Jolene watched him walk the last few steps to the house and heard the soft clink as he unlocked the door. How often had Grandpa gone back wishing he could change things? Had he tried to keep Uncle George from the war? Had he tried to prevent Grandma from dying? It must have been so heartbreaking. No wonder he was exhausted, so worn with emotion, when he returned.

Inside, Grandpa read the local paper and busied himself tidying up. Jolene curled up on the couch with a book, but she was having a hard time reading. She could see Grandpa growing restless. Finally, he got up and stood in front of the living room window. "I think I'll take a little walk."

"Down Dominion Avenue? Can I come, please?" She bounced off the couch.

Grandpa studied her, his dark green eyes reading hers in silence. "All right," he agreed finally, "but remember, you can't change history."

Chapter Seven

"Phew!" said Jolene, looking into the hollow tree trunk and extracting her boy's clothes. "They're still here." They pulled on their borrowed clothing, Jolene wondering what adventure awaited her in her disguise.

Together they walked into town. A late afternoon wind blew spring around. Just outside the stable, a wagon stood, piled high with shiny black lumps of coal. "They must be making the rounds," observed Grandpa. "Delivering coal to the houses."

As he spoke, a man clambered up into the wagon. He smiled at them, his teeth flashing white in a coal-dusted face.

Grandpa waved. "Now that's a dirty job."

"I'll say! Says something for natural gas, don't you think?"

"Hey Jo!" Daniel raced out from behind a miner's cottage holding a long, wooden stick. "I was just going fishing. Want to come along?"

"Can I?" Jolene looked hopefully at Grandpa.

"All right," said Grandpa. "Be polite and stay together. I'll head uptown."

Jolene joined Daniel, marvelling at their ability to run about town. Her mother would never have allowed her this freedom in Calgary. Daniel was carrying a willow switch, with a piece of string knotted to the top, from which a pin was suspended. "Is that your fishing rod?" Jolene asked, picturing her uncle's fancy graphite one in Calgary.

"Yep, and I got me some bait, too." Daniel reached into his pocket and pulled out a bunch of red wool.

Jolene bit her tongue and wondered what her uncle would say if she suggested red wool in place of one of his elaborate fishing flies. She followed Daniel towards the railway.

He balanced on a single rail. "Bet you can't do this," he said, spinning a full 360 degrees on one foot, then wobbling slightly before falling off onto the wooden ties.

Jolene smirked. The rails were almost as wide as a balance beam, but her boots were much slicker than her bare feet. She held her arms steady and spun, rotating quickly back into her original position. Then she spun again, in the opposite direction, perfectly balanced.

"You're good at that," said Daniel. "What else can you do?"

Mentally, Jolene rehearsed her balance beam routine. She ran a few steps, sailed into a cartwheel and caught herself on the rail. Daniel let out a low, appreciative whistle. He stood staring at her for a moment, wonder in his eyes.

A sparrow twittered in a nearby tree and, as if taking a cue, they raced towards the river. "My fishing hole's along here," said Daniel. He picked his way down the bank to a deep blue bend in the river. "Caught me a big trout last year." He held his arms about a metre apart.

Jolene laughed. She'd heard dozens of fish stories in her lifetime. "I don't believe that for a minute. There's no trout that big."

"Is so!" Daniel searched the shadows. "Look! There's one now."

Jolene turned just in time to see a big splash of water.

"Did you see him jump? That's about the size of the one I caught."

Jolene squinted into the slashes of light that pierced the deep pool. From the size of the ripples, there was no doubt that it had been a huge fish. "You caught one that big?" she asked. Daniel nodded. Jolene scrutinized the river just as another splash sounded. A fuzzy back dove under the water, followed by a broad, flat tail. "Hey, that was no fish!" she protested. "That was a beaver slapping its tail!"

Daniel leaned his fishing pole against a tree and chuckled. Another slap on the water made them both jump.

"Come on," he urged. "That beaver's dammed the river

up yonder. If we jimmy her dam, maybe she'll come fix it."
Jolene followed him to the dam. Tangles of logs packed
together with mud made an impressive barrier on the river.
They pulled apart the logs on the edge of it, allowing them
to float downstream. Then they hid behind some bushes on
the bank and watched.

A few minutes later, Daniel pointed to the black nose of
the beaver in the water. Already she had reclaimed one of
the floating logs and was swimming upstream to replace it.
Jolene watched the beaver make her repairs swiftly and effi-
ciently. "Sweet!" she breathed.

Daniel looked at her with that same look of wonder he'd
given her earlier and Jolene checked herself. She had to
remember what time period she was in.

"Where do you come from anyway?" he asked her.

She could hardly tell him that she was from the future.
"Calgary."

"You came by train, then?"

"Uh . . . "

Luckily, Daniel was more interested in telling her his
story than hearing hers. "Pa came first for the opening of
the town. He liked it, so we eventually moved here." He
skipped a stone across the water and the beaver dove. "I'd
have rather gone to the city."

Jolene sat in silence, her thoughts rippling like the river
below her. It was funny how you came to live in places, how
your family's decisions shaped your life. And, Jolene de-

cided, it was important to know about those things, too.

"Come on," said Daniel, picking up his fishing pole. "I'll show you another good spot."

They pushed through a clump of wild rose bushes that tore at their trousers, bent under a branchy bush that almost stole Jolene's cap and arrived at a trail on the bank of the river. Silver water glistened in the depressions of rocks. Grasses, still groggy with winter, stretched across their path. The river bubbled happily. Jolene inhaled spring.

As they rounded a bend, a soggy golden-coloured dog darted out of the water, barking. "Peaches, what'cha doing here?" Daniel rubbed the dog's ears and Peaches wagged her tail happily. "She's Old Man Warner's," he explained. "He's this old trapper who camps down near the river. Lives in a tent all summer long and all winter too, with just old Peaches here for company. Come on, we'll take her home and you can meet him."

Jolene followed, wondering what a real trapper would be like. She didn't have to wonder for long. Ahead, standing in the river, his pants rolled to his knees, was a grizzly old man who looked like something in a history book. He bent down and splashed a handful of water onto his face. Maybe he was already in a history book. She'd have to check.

Peaches let out a deep growl. The old trapper straightened up and wiped the water from his eyes. "Why ye old traitor," he said to the dog. "Don't ye recognize yer own master?" Peaches bounded towards the voice. The grizzly man ruffled the dog's fur, rinsed his hands in the water and picked his way across the rocks towards the shore. "Ye didn't know me, did ye, dawg? All this spit and polish."

He dried himself with his shirt as Jolene and Daniel approached him. "Young Daniel," he called, catching sight of them. "It's been a while since I've seen ye. And who be yer friend there?"

"This is Jo. Him and his grandpa just arrived."

Old Man Warner pulled the flannel shirt that had just served as a towel over his undershirt and rolled down his pant legs. "Ah, and where do ye come from, Jo?"

"Calgary."

"A city boy, hey!" The old trapper pulled on his wool socks and boots. "There," he said, standing and wringing out his beard. He placed a soiled, brown hat on his head and straightened up stiffly. "That there water's still a mite cold, but I expect I'm a sight more respectable now."

He grinned proudly and Jolene, smothering a laugh, noticed his near-toothless gums. Beside him, Peaches shook, splattering the old trapper with muddy water. Daniel and Jolene laughed out loud.

"Come on back to my place while I warm up a bit. It's a mite cold, but then I suppose it ain't yet May."

They followed him towards a tent set metres back from the river. Off to the side was a firepit with a chopping block and a neat pile of wood. Jolene shuddered at the thought of camping year round. It was cold in the mountains and she was pretty sure that the old trapper didn't own an insulated sleeping bag. In a stand of trees nearby, half a dozen pelts — brown, red, silver, black, grey — hung lifeless from the branches. "Yuck!" she murmured, as a wave of nausea passed over her.

Daniel followed her gaze. "Don't tell me you're going to go and get all squeamish like some girl," he whispered.

"Can ye stay for a history lesson?" asked Old Man Warner, poking at some embers in the firepit. He reached into the tent, hauled out a patch of fur and handed it to Daniel. "Here ye go, sit yerselves down on that."

Jolene stared at the cratered eye sockets and leathery nose and tried to calm her stomach. Bit by bit, she seated herself next to Daniel.

"So Daniel," prompted Old Man Warner, sitting on a polished log, "which story would ye like today?"

"Guess!"

The trapper snorted loudly and clapped his gnarled hands together. "So be it then — the lost Lemon Mine." He fingered the handle of the ax stuck in a chopping block next to him, rolled up a sleeve and glanced at the sun washing over the mountain. Jolene followed his gaze. A funny feeling filled her gut. She turned away from Turtle Mountain, back to the old trapper. "'Twas the spring of 1873," he began, his voice pushing aside the silence. "Maybe on a day such as this one." Beside her, Daniel settled into the wolf skin and the story. Despite her misgivings, Jolene leaned forward to listen.

"Two men, one named Lemon and the other called

Blackjack went looking for gold." The old trapper chuckled. "Lots of men went looking for gold in them days, but there was a big party this time and Lemon and Blackjack had money backing them. So they loaded up their horses with supplies and headed out. Blackjack, he was one of the best gold diggers around in them days. Shame about what happened to him."

Jolene looked expectantly at Old Man Warner, but he merely went on with his story. "Lemon, Blackjack and the others, they travelled in a big group for protection from the Blackfeet. Many a man looking for gold was killed by the Blackfeet in them days. They could sneak up behind any man without him knowing." Jolene watched the trapper's gnarled hands pad silently through the air. "Could get right close to him on those silent moccasins and then . . ." A knife flashed in the old man's hand. Jolene shrieked. Daniel laughed. Old Man Warner chuckled. His voice was deep and throaty. "Ye laugh young Daniel, but before ye knew it, there'd be a scalp dangling from a pole and a man's gold digging days were done."

"Is that what happened to Blackjack?" Jolene's voice trembled.

The trapper shook his head before continuing. "A few weeks into the trip, the party split. Blackjack and Lemon followed an old lodge-pole trail up the High River towards Tobacco Plains. The others headed towards Stand Off. Blackjack and Lemon found showings in the river."

"Showings?" Jolene was puzzled.

"Traces of gold when they were panning. They followed the mountain stream upwards towards the headwaters and struck gold. Right there and then, they sank two pits. And then, then they got really lucky. While they were bringing in their packhorses, they found the ledge, the ledge containing the gold. They say there was so much gold in that rock that it sparkled like the northern lights."

Old Man Warner paused and a smoky grey cloud shadowed the sun. "That night, in camp, Lemon and Blackjack argued. Lemon wanted to stay on and Blackjack wanted to come back in the spring — file a claim and then return. As the night wore on and the whiskey flowed, things got worse and worse." Old Man Warner got to his feet and stood behind the log. "For half the night, they argued, threatened each other with their fists and screamed curses through the darkness. Finally, Blackjack would talk about it no more. Refused to say another word. Crawled into his sleeping roll and fell asleep."

Jolene licked her lips and swallowed hard.

"But Lemon, all he could think about was having to leave the camp and wait until the spring to claim the gold. The more he thought about it, the more his mind raged, until, in the night, black as a crow's tail feather, he sneaked past his partner towards the fire."

Old Man Warner crept behind them and circled back towards the firepit, as silent as a deer going down to the water. His hands reached out towards the ax handle and lifted it out of the chopping block. "In the glow of the moonlight, Lemon seized the ax, slunk towards his sleeping partner and with a single blow, killed Blackjack." The ax swept downward in a loud thud, sinking its blade deep into the chopping block.

Jolene jumped. The old trapper turned towards them, his eyes flashing in the shadows. His voice was soft now. "And then, only then, did Lemon realize what he'd done. Killed his partner. Murdered Blackjack in cold blood." His words clung to Jolene's skin.

"His first thought was to leave, to run, but everywhere he turned, there was the face of Blackjack calling his name — 'Lemon, Lemon.' Cold fingers reached out and touched him. Scared to death, he built a raging fire. He didn't dare sleep. Instead, he slung his gun over his shoulder and paced back and forth beside the flames, back and forth through the night."

The old trapper resettled himself on his polished log and grinned. "Must have been something to see." He glanced up at them. "And he was seen. For tho' he didn't know it, two Stoney braves had followed them. And they seen everything — the gold, the murder — they seen it all. All night long, they howled like wolves, whistled, moaned and called Lemon's name, making him half-crazed with guilt."

Jolene's eyes were two moons. "What did he do?"

"At the first hint o' morning, he took his horse and set off on a trail across the mountains. He left the body and the camp, but he took the gold. The two Stoney braves took the rest of the horses and set off for Morley where they told their old chief everything."

The sun edged out from behind the cloud. "The old chief, he was frightened by the braves' story. Scared that if news of the gold strike got out, the white men would run thick as ants over the Stoney's hunting grounds. So he swore the two braves to silence. He put a curse on them if they ever told anyone about the gold or the camp."

Peaches settled at Jolene's feet. She reached out and rubbed the dog's belly, glad of its soft warmth. "Ye can imagine what a stir it caused when Lemon showed up at Tobacco Plains with the gold. There was many a man who would have set off on the spot with him, but he was raving mad by then. They sent a priest to talk to him and he confessed everything. The priest sent a mountain man to find the body and camp. He found it all right, buried Blackjack and built a mound of stones to keep the wolves away. Then he headed back to Tobacco Plains. But no sooner had he left the camp than the braves returned, tore down the stones and scattered 'em everywhere. Left nothing, not a trace."

Old Man Warner scratched at a spot in his beard. "Many's the man who's tried to find that spot since and many's the man who's paid the price for looking."

"The curse?" asked Jolene.

Old Man Warner shrugged. "Mysterious fatal illnesses, deadly fires — there's no explaining some things."

"Did they ever find the gold?"

"Not yet, tho' there's lots that believe it's still out there."

Daniel's eyes gleamed. "Wouldn't you like to try, Jo? I mean, how would it be to find the lost Lemon Mine?"

"Is it around here then?"

"Some say that this is the area," said Old Man Warner.

A shrill whistle cut the air. Daniel jumped up, pulled Jolene to her feet and out of Old Man Warner's tale. "Come on, Jo. I've got chores to do." He smiled at the old trapper. "Can we come back again?"

The trapper laughed from somewhere deep in his belly. "That ye can, Daniel and Jo, too — come for another history lesson."

They thanked Old Man Warner, picked up Daniel's fishing rod, gave Peaches a belly rub and started back down the river trail. "That was a history lesson?" said Jolene, more to herself than Daniel.

Daniel chuckled. "He's the oldest man in town. He's lived through so much that he's kind of like living history, I guess."

Living history. It was no wonder he made the past seem so vibrant and exciting. Jolene sighed. It was too bad that Dad couldn't do the same in his museum.

"Ma always says that he tells history as his story, you know *his story*." Daniel split the word in half.

She'd never thought about the word *history* before, but, of course, it was right there — the story in history. It was as much a part of history as all the facts and dates and details she'd had to memorize this year.

Daniel picked up the pace and changed the subject. "I hate chores," he grumbled. "Ma's always after me to chop kindling or refill the lamps and it's always cutting into my fishing time."

"I know what you mean," said Jolene, envisioning her job list posted on the fridge. She stopped short of complaining about having to vacuum the upstairs or unload the dishwasher.

"That's the trouble with parents," said Daniel. "They don't remember what it's like to be young."

Jolene thought about her last day of school and how embarrassed she'd been handing out Dad's museum coupons. Had nothing changed after one hundred years?

"Come on," called Daniel, breaking into a trot.

Before long their feet were pounding down a dirt path into town. They raced past a church, and then stopped in front of a fancy, two-storey stone building. "That's the school," Daniel told Jolene. "Just built. My class is upstairs." He pointed to one of the second-storey windows in the left wing. "You comin' tomorrow? What standard are you in, anyway?" But Daniel didn't wait for an answer. "I'm in standard seven. I'll be fourteen in September."

Jolene would be thirteen in the fall and had just completed grade six. It seemed like years ago now. "I'm in seven too," she said. "Guess we'd be in the same class."

"At least for a few months," said Daniel. "Pa's trying to get me a job with the mine. If he does, I won't go back to school next year."

Jolene stood motionless, stunned by his words. "But you'll only be fourteen. You can't work in the mine!"

"I know that," retorted Daniel. "I'd start on the surface at the tipple. Then, when I'm sixteen or at least tall enough to look sixteen, I'd go underground."

Jolene recalled her visit to the Bellevue mine, how it had felt to be swallowed up by the darkness inside the guts of the mountain. "But it's so dark and damp and cold and smothering underground. Aren't you scared?"

Daniel scrutinized her, a perplexed look settling over his face. "No, I ain't scared. Being scared's for girls." He paused. "You say the oddest things sometimes."

Jolene pulled her cap securely down on her head and looked away. She had to remember that she was masquerading as a boy. She had to be brave and take risks.

"It's not the best place in the world to work," Daniel admitted, "but it'd be nice to help Pa earn some extra money. Anyway, I'll probably start out at the picking tables."

Jolene tried to imagine Daniel sorting coal, the creases of his hands stained black like his father's. From there he would go underground, deep inside the mountain, into the rooms and the dusty, explosive blackness. "Don't you like school?" she asked. Daniel didn't answer.

Jolene bit her bottom lip. It probably wasn't cool to admit that you liked school in 1903. Or maybe that was a girl thing to do. Suddenly, she didn't care. "I like school," she said boldly, bracing herself for Daniel's reaction.

He said nothing at first. "Really?" he asked cautiously. "You like school?"

Jolene felt the colour creep into her cheeks, but that didn't matter. She did like school. "Most of the time," she admitted. "And I'm a good student, too." She waited for his scornful reply.

His voice was low and even when he spoke. "I like school, too," he admitted. "And I'm good at it as well — got straight A's all year." Jolene could hear the pride in his voice. She looked up and smiled broadly at him. His hazel eyes were distant and dreamy. "I want to be a barrister one day and work for the union — make sure the miners have good working conditions, negotiate good contracts."

"But then you have to finish school and go on to study law. Don't your parents know that?"

Daniel's dreamy look disappeared. "No, and I don't dare tell them. Pa doesn't believe in all that book stuff they teach us in school. He says that if I can read and write and do a bit of math, that's all I need." He sighed. "Ma's keener to keep me in school, but even she admits that the extra money would help."

Jolene stared at the schoolhouse. How many times had she listened to her parents tell her how important it was to get an education? And now, Daniel wanted one and his parents were the ones standing in his way.

"Come on," called Daniel, waving his fishing rod at her. "We'll find your grandpa and then I'd best get home for chores." His long steps turned the corner and thudded onto a wooden boardwalk.

They had reached Dominion Avenue and Jolene stared down the main street of Frank. Flat-faced buildings lined the boardwalk, which in turn lined a broad, dirt road. Horses, their tails flicking, stood tied to hitching posts. Wagons rolled down the road, dust billowing behind them. Jolene followed Daniel past the old-fashioned storefronts, trying to take it all in. Our photographs will always whisper, "Come again" claimed a sign in the window of Crown Studios. "Meals at all times" promised the Palm Restaurant. A group of women in long dresses and hats skirted past them. Jolene watched them over her shoulder. Suddenly, she bumped into a dark three-piece suit.

"Hmmph!" declared a gruff voice. "Should have known it would be the likes of you, Daniel MacEachern." The eyes above the voice narrowed.

"Afternoon, Mr. Barrett." Daniel looked around nervously. "I . . . I should be going. Got to refill the lamps before supper." The man followed them with his eyes.

"He's the bank manager," Daniel whispered to Jolene as they scurried down the boardwalk. "Some say he's got four loaded revolvers under his desk and he'd use 'em, too." Jolene glanced back over her shoulder, trying to imprint Mr. Barrett's face on her mind. He was one person she definitely planned to avoid.

They ducked past a crowd of men emerging from the

Imperial Hotel, and for a brief moment, Jolene caught a glimpse of glasses shimmering in the reflection of a mirror. The smell of whiskey swirled above the boardwalk. Daniel hesitated beside the group of men. "Excuse me, Mr. Cornel, sir," he said, laying a hand gently on the woolen arm of a dark-skinned man. "We're looking for Jo's grandpa, Victor Basso. He's new in town. Do you know if he's here?"

Mr. Cornel frowned, his eyes glassy and thoughtful. "Didn't see anybody but the regular town folk, lad. Might try the Union or Frank Hotel."

Daniel muttered his thanks and traipsed down the boardwalk. Jolene scrambled to catch up with him. They couldn't just march into a bar, could they? Wasn't there a legal drinking age?

A pretty young woman, accompanied by an older version of herself, walked towards them. "Good day, Daniel," said the older woman. "Do tell your ma to drop by for tea, won't you?"

"I will, ma'am," Daniel replied, then nodded towards the younger woman who was dressed in a long, navy skirt and white shawl. She glanced up at them. Jolene was startled by the brightness of her green eyes. The two women moved on. "She's crazy," whispered Daniel. "The younger one, I mean. She sees things that don't exist."

Jolene whirled around. That was Aunt Peggy — that woman with the brilliant eyes.

Chapter Eight

If only Jolene could find a way to talk to Peggy or Peggy's father. Her great-great-grandfather had written the journal that Grandpa had found. He might be able to explain exactly how the time creases worked. "Have you ever met Peggy's father?" Jolene asked Daniel, but he had already stepped past three tethered horses, propped his fishing rod near the door of a shop and disappeared inside.

Jolene's eyes swept upwards. GENERAL STORE read the sign in the window. At least it wasn't the saloon. She followed Daniel inside.

Grandpa's voice was the first one she heard. He was sitting beside the stove, surrounded by an attentive circle of men. He was, she knew by the feeling in the room, telling a story. A wave of laughter flooded the store and she moved closer on Daniel's heels. Grandpa looked up, caught her eye and motioned for her to join him, but she hung back on the edge of his words.

"Up north, we used to go out hunting for mountain goat quite a bit," began Grandpa. Jolene shot a puzzled look at him. Grandpa had never been a hunter, never liked shooting animals at all. "There was this one big, old goat — so big and so old that his coat had yellowed in the moonlight. For it was always in the moonlight that we'd see him, standing on top of a mountain peak, his horns tipped with stars."

"I'd better be on my way," said Daniel, leaning closer to Grandpa's voice and settling into the circle.

Jolene smiled. Grandpa had that effect on people.

"My buddy, Jimmy, he was determined to get this old mountain goat. So one cold, blustery day, we headed out, way up in the mountains, sweeping the peaks, looking for the moon goat. We spread out across the valley, agreed to meet back at camp at the end of the day. So me, I'm climbin' high up on this peak, and the wind, she's whipping into me. So strong that I can't get around to the front face. So I climb up even higher and I find myself a ledge, about a foot wide, and if it doesn't wrap right round to the rocky front face of the mountain. I sling my rifle criss-crossed over my shoulder and I start out onto the ledge."

Grandpa's eyes circled the room. "But the wind, she's really howling now and the ledge is getting narrow and crumbly, so I reckon that the thing to do is to get down on my hands and knees and crawl. It's slow going, but it's working and I'm thinking maybe I'll be able to spot that big, old goat from the front face of the mountain. Maybe I'll even get a shot at him. So I keep crawling head down against the wind, and when I look up, there's the moon goat, on the same ledge, standing so close I can almost reach out and touch him." Grandpa's hand reached through the air. "Seems he came around from the other side of the peak — walked the same ledge that I crawled from the other direction."

A couple of the men snickered and Grandpa paused. Jolene studied the group around him, bodies hunched forward over his words, over the neglected checkers board in their midst. It was hard to imagine that he'd once been scared to speak in public, once pretended that his listeners were horses.

"So there I am on my hands and knees and right in front of me is this big, old moon goat, just standing there, watching me. And I can't believe my luck, can't believe it for a minute. Only I can't reach back and grab my rifle, because if I do, sure as anything, I'll fall off the ledge and it's a long, rocky slope down to the valley. And the moon goat, he ain't moving — after all, it's his mountain. And so we stay like that for a bit, both of us on all fours, frozen on that ledge high on the mountain."

Grandpa played with his moustache. "In the end, I figure that there's only one thing to do. I start crawling backwards, backing out along the ledge on my hands and knees, back off that front face. And all the time, I'm hoping that when I get off the ledge and down below the peak, that old goat will still be standing there, his horns dripping with stars. But of course he ain't. He's long gone, chasing the moon somewhere."

The door to the store opened and two women clattered in. The shopkeeper behind the counter nodded briefly and leaned back into Grandpa's story.

"So I'm walking back, cursing my luck, dumb luck, all the way back to camp and when I get there, Jimmy's sitting stock still, his head resting against this big, prickly spruce tree. He's got a good campfire going, though it's burnt down some already and right away, I launch into my story. Jimmy there, he keeps raising one hand, trying to interrupt, but I can't stop talkin', gotta' tell my story and the words are just spilling out of me. And finally Jimmy stops trying to get my attention and just sits there, not moving, not moving at all. And pretty soon, I notice that Jimmy ain't moving and I stop yakking. Turns out that Jimmy's hair is stuck, glued to the sap of this big, old spruce, heated by the fire before he fell asleep, and now hardened, hard as glue."

Laughter shattered the store's stillness. Daniel's grin stretched from ear to ear and Grandpa's eyes were bright and alive. Grandpa cleared his throat. "Had to cut his hair free with my hunting knife, I did. And all I had to show for the trip when I got back home was holes in the knees of my pants. And Jimmy, well, he'd got a story to tell the barber."

Always a story, another story to tell. Jolene couldn't ask Grandpa to stop telling his stories, even if Mom and Dad thought he was losing his mind.

The men straightened up, the shopkeeper turned his attention to the ladies that had just come in and Daniel, taking one look at the darkening sky, moved to the door. "I'd better be getting on home," said Daniel as he passed Jolene. "Maybe I'll see you at school tomorrow?"

"Maybe." Jolene watched Daniel leave and then looked around. The chatter of languages she didn't recognize filled the store. She focused her attention on the two women at the counter. "And I also need lye," said the younger one. "All that coal dust seeps into everything. I don't think I'll ever get used to it." She ran her hand across a bolt of material.

"You will, believe me," said the older woman, pulling a loose thread off her long-sleeved taffy-coloured dress. Tiny buttons held her cuffs and secured a small slit in the neckline. Her shoes laced up the front and had small, square heels. "It's the laundry going stiff on the line, and the eggs and milk freezing in the cupboard that I thought I'd never get used to, but I did." She removed her hat and Jolene studied her rounded, rolled hair with interest. "That and the three long whistles of the mine," she said solemnly. The younger woman winced.

Jolene knew that three long whistles meant there'd been an accident at the mine.

"Well, I hope I never hear them," said the younger woman. Her dark skirt hung almost to her shoes and was cinched and belted at the waist. A high-necked ivory blouse, with a lacy collar and long sleeves was tucked in to ironed pleats. She had a foreign accent that Jolene couldn't place.

In front of her on the counter, the shopkeeper was weighing onions on a large silver scale. Tins lined the upper shelves behind him and in the waning light, Jolene could just make out their contents: lard, sweet milk, salt, halibut liver oil capsules, corn pads and cough drops. Boxes followed the cans: wooden cheese boxes, biscuit boxes, and tobacco boxes stretched all the way to the bearskin mounted on the wall. Starch, ammonia, brushes, china, bowls and thread occupied the shelves.

"Shall we go?" asked Grandpa, coming up behind Jolene.

"Do we have to?"

"A person would think that you like it here in the good old days."

Jolene mulled over that thought. A lot of things had changed during the last century. She wasn't convinced that she'd rather live in 1903, but there were good things about these days, too.

The sun had set and the air was cool and shivery. They meandered their way down Dominion Avenue. She looked around her at the shops and offices as they passed them — the watchmaker's shop and the newspaper office.

"I wonder what made the news today?" mused Grandpa.

"A bear sighting or a wagon swept away by a torrential spring river?" They strolled past the cigar shop, the laundry and the post office. "Or who got a letter from abroad? Was there a child born under lucky stars?"

Were there really lucky stars? Had Michael been born under lucky stars? Jolene was only six minutes older than he was. Surely, she'd been born under those same stars.

"Look," said Grandpa pointing across the street, "there's the good doctor. Isn't that what you want to be?" A grey-haired man with a stethoscope hanging around his neck locked the door of an office and started down the board-walk.

"It is," said Jolene, "although I'm not sure I'd want to be a doctor in 1903." She could only imagine what medicines they didn't have yet. "Daniel wants to be a lawyer," Jolene told Grandpa, "but his dad wants him to quit school and work at the tipple next year."

"That's not uncommon for 1903."

"But it's not fair. Daniel doesn't want to be a miner. And if he'd lived a century later, he wouldn't even be allowed to work at McDonald's yet."

Grandpa smiled at her. "People's attitudes towards children and education have changed a lot in the last hundred years, Jo."

"Then there has to be a way to change Daniel's parents' attitude!"

Grandpa put an arm around her shoulders. "You can try,"

he said, "but remember this isn't the twenty-first century."

Jolene didn't need Grandpa to remind her of that. They passed the cottages, crossed Gold Creek and walked down the road beside the livery stable. Near the construction camp, they turned onto the railway track, their feet keeping the rhythm of the wooden ties. In a boxcar on a sideline, children scrambled about. "Look," said Grandpa pointing to the car, "they're sweeping out the box car, collecting grain for the chickens. I bet their favourites will come flapping over to them when they get home."

One small boy was not participating. He sat off to the side, peering up at the letters on the side of the boxcar. Grandpa chuckled. "See that little guy, over there," he said, pointing to the small boy. "He reminds me of your father when he was young. He was always so preoccupied with details."

That, Jolene decided, was the difference between her grandfather and her father. Grandpa saw the stories. Dad saw the letters.

Soon they reached the grove of trees and changed clothes before continuing across the field towards the river.

"Can you see the time crease?" asked Grandpa as the erratic became visible.

Even in the growing darkness, Jolene could make out the dense shadow of the time crease. "Can I try?" she asked. Grandpa nodded. She took a deep breath and shut her eyes. "I'm fixed at a point in space letting time pass over me." She felt a momentary hot breeze, a feeling of tension, and opened her eyes. They were still firmly situated beside the erratic in 1903.

"It takes practice," said Grandpa, taking her hand. He closed his eyes, his forehead wrinkling as a result of his concentration. In moments they had staggered through the time crease.

Back at the house, Jolene helped Grandpa prepare supper. When they had eaten, Grandpa sat down in a big easy chair with the newspaper. Within minutes, he was asleep. The phone rang and Jolene grabbed it before it could wake him. It was Dad wondering how they were doing.

"We're both fine, Dad."

"What did you do today? I phoned earlier, but nobody was in."

Jolene contemplated his question. She could hardly tell him about the beaver, Old Man Warner, the general store, the banker with his four loaded revolvers! "We just poked around," she said finally.

"I'm going to be an extra day in Calgary, Jolene," said Dad. "There are a few things that need attending to here."

"That's okay, Dad." Jolene's heart skipped at the possibility of being able to visit Frank again the next day.

"And Grandpa is fine, Jolene? He hasn't been telling any stories has he?"

"He's perfectly fine," she assured him, choosing to answer only his first question. "I'm sure that you and Mom are worried about nothing."

"I hope you're right," said Dad.

"I am." Jolene took a deep breath. "Gramps has such a good imagination that when he tells stories, he makes them seem so real. I think that's why he mixes things up sometimes."

"It's important to understand the difference between fiction and reality."

"I know," agreed Jolene. She longed to tell Dad that Grandpa had discovered a way to step back into the history that both of them loved. But that would only complicate matters.

"We have to ensure that he's not a danger to himself or anyone else."

Jolene wondered how they'd do that. Would they put him in a home? The thought made her shudder. "He's not, Dad," Jolene assured him. If only she could find a way to explain Grandpa's odd behaviour.

"We'll talk more later," said Dad. "I'll see you the day after tomorrow." Jolene hung up the phone. She stood, for a long time, gazing out into the twilight at the outline of the slide. Then she walked across the room and stood looking at Grandpa, asleep in his chair. Maybe she couldn't change history, but Grandpa's life wasn't history, at least not yet. Perhaps, just perhaps, she could find a way to change that.

Chapter Nine

"Hey Jo, hurry up," called Daniel as Jolene and Grandpa arrived at the miners' cottages. "Hurry up, or we'll be late for school."

"School?" asked Jolene. She looked up at her grandfather. "Should I go?"

"It's your choice," said Grandpa, studying her.

Jolene looked from Grandpa to Daniel. "Why not?" she said. After all, she was supposed to be a risk-taker and school in 1903 sounded pretty risky to her.

"Off you go then," said Grandpa, a smile crossing his lips.

Jolene joined Daniel in a brisk walk. "Our teacher, Miss Trudell, is real nice," he told her. "And pretty, too. Lots of the young miners got an eye for her."

Jolene did not respond. Her mind raced ahead of her feet. School in 1903? A bell rang and they ran towards the big, two-storey stone building they had seen earlier. Daniel flung open the heavy door and raced up a flight of stairs. Jolene followed him down a central corridor, past the cloakrooms and some classrooms. He slowed to a walk as they reached the final door at the end of the corridor, removed his cap and stuffed it into his pocket.

Jolene hesitated. Without her cap, she might look like a girl. She took a deep breath, pulled it off and flattened her hair against her head. That was a chance she'd have to take.

"Come in, Daniel," said the teacher, smiling at him. Her eyes reached Jolene. "And I see we have yet another new student!"

"This is Jo, Miss Trudell."

Jolene stared at the young woman Daniel had addressed. She was tall, slim and so young, so very young. She couldn't have been more than nineteen years old. "Hello, Jo. We'll have to get another desk for you. In the meantime, Samuel's absent today so you can use his for now."

Daniel pointed to a shiny honey-coloured desk with iron legs and a double seat across the aisle from his own. Another boy was already seated on one side of the seat. Jolene slid into the too-small seat beside him as the teacher's voice slid through the attendance register. Chalk-yellow daffodils and violet-faced pansies bordered the chalkboard at the front of the room. A stately man stared down from a framed picture. Squinting, Jolene could just make out the inscription below it: King Edward VII.

"Present!" said a voice beside her. Jolene jumped, and for

the first time, looked at the boy seated next to her. Waves of thick black hair beat against the boy's forehead. His eyes were the colour of the sea, his skin the hue of driftwood bleached in the sun.

"And Jo," said Miss Trudell," adding a name to the bottom of the register. "What's your family name, Jo?"

Jolene's head shot up. "Basso," she stammered. Miss Trudell wrote it in the register, placed her straight pen back in the inkwell and stood up.

The class rose and Jolene rose, too, banging her knees on the shelf beneath her desktop. She lost her balance and fell towards the boy with whom she shared a seat. He put out a hand to steady her and she righted herself. She looked down, a scarlet blush creeping up her throat. Like all the other students, she angled her body towards the front of the room.

A large red, white and blue flag, which she recognized as the old Union Jack flag of England, hung ceremoniously above the chalkboard. Below it hung a crucifix. Miss Trudell raised a hand and began to make the sign of the cross. "In the name of the Father, the Son and the Holy Spirit." The class began to recite the Lord's Prayer and Jolene followed along. As soon as the prayer was done, the students sat down. Jolene slid into her seat, bumping the elbow of the boy beside her. Ocean-blue eyes brimmed over thick black eyelashes. He grinned at her.

Jolene held her breath. She was unnerved by the way he looked right at her. Leaning forward, he tugged at the bow of the blond girl in front of them who turned her head to half-scowl, half-smile in his direction. He shifted towards Jolene until his leg touched hers, making her heart pound. "That's Edna. She likes me," he whispered with a slight accent Jolene couldn't place.

"Robert!" came Miss Trudell's stern warning. She glared at the boy beside Jolene. "Nobody gave you permission to speak. And you boys stop bothering Edna."

Robert straightened up and Jolene grew tense in her chair, feeling a mixture of relief and disappointment. Of course! Robert thought she was a boy. Why wouldn't he? She was supposed to be a boy. She had a boy's name and boy's clothes. She contemplated the bright green bow that held the bouncy curls of the girl in front of her. It matched the girl's green cotton dress with its long sleeves and brass buttons. Jolene strained to see what she was wearing on her feet. They were ankle high shoes into which were tucked plain black, probably itchy, stockings. Jolene rubbed her heels together, glad of her comfortable clothing. She stole another look at the handsome face beside her and then at Daniel's studious one.

"We will begin with geography," announced Miss Trudell, picking up her wooden pointer and indicating a map on the wall. "Who can tell me what this region is called?" She indicated the landmass along the western coast of Canada. Across the aisle from Jolene, Daniel raised his hand. "Yes, Daniel."

"British Columbia."

"And this area directly to the east?" Miss Trudell looked around. "Jo?"

"Uh, Alberta," stammered Jolene, wondering why there were lines drawn through the province.

"The entire area," prompted Miss Trudell. She swept what appeared to be the province of Alberta with her pointer.

Jolene looked helplessly at Daniel. "The province of Alberta," she said timidly.

The class giggled. Beside her, Robert stifled a smile. Miss Trudell marched deliberately down the aisle until she stood in front of Jolene's desk. The end of her pointer came to rest on Jolene's collarbone beneath her jacket. "In this school, Jo Basso, we do not tolerate such back talk," she said sternly. "You are, like everybody else in this room, aware that we do not live in a province, but in a territory, and you will tell us the name of that territory." She turned on her heel and walked purposefully to the front of the classroom. The silence in the room lengthened with each step.

Jolene shot a desperate look at Daniel. He mouthed something to her, but she could not make it out. Miss Trudell had reached the teacher's desk and stood waiting. Jolene took a deep breath, spun the wheel in her mind and chose a territory from the three she knew. "Northwest Territories," she stammered.

"Which is divided into four provisional districts," continued Miss Trudell.

Jolene sighed with relief and sank down into her seat. Alberta hadn't become a province until 1905, she recalled too late. She would have to be more careful, more careful and more silent.

"To our north is the Athabasca district," said Miss Trudell indicating the northern portion of Alberta. "What resources are we likely to find in that area?" Jolene shrank down even further. But that proved to be a bad tactic. "Sit up please, Jo and answer the question."

Jolene pulled herself upright. Her face burned and she willed herself to think. Oil and gas would come later. "Trees," she murmured, "lots of trees."

"Correct! The Athabascan region is heavily wooded." Miss Trudell's voice droned on about the resources and landforms of the region.

"And now you may pair up with the person beside you and prepare for the geography spelling bee after recess."

Robert dug out an atlas and leaned into Jolene, his shoulder rubbing up against hers. "We want Edna on our team," he told her. She looked away. "Athabasca," he read, giving her the first spelling word.

By the time the recess bell rang, Jolene's face was flushed and she was in need of air. She was also in need of a toilet. "Where's the bathroom?" she asked Daniel as they headed down the stairs.

"The what?" he asked, throwing open the door and stepping into the sunshine.

A group of girls and boys stood around two wooden out-houses at the edge of the schoolyard. Jolene motioned in their direction and they crossed the dirt field together. She lined up behind a girl with frilly sleeves. Daniel snickered. "You aimin' to use the girls'?" he asked. Jolene blushed and changed lines. There were too many things to remember when you'd come from the future to the past, when you were a girl who was supposed to be a boy.

After recess, Jolene sat very still and straight, trying to listen, trying not to attract attention to herself. Miss Trudell was discussing grammar — verbs and adverbs. Beside her, Robert fiddled with the straight pen in the groove at the top of their desk. Jolene's eyes wandered to the middle of their desk, to the blue pot of ink there. She reached out a finger and touched the clay pot. Miss Trudell was talking and handing out scribblers at the same time. She placed a blank one on the desk in front of Jolene, returned to the chalk-board and began to write.

The room buzzed as students reached for their pens. Jolene looked around. There were a lot of students — almost fifty of them and only one teacher. She thought of her mom's reaction when she had told her that they had a class of thirty-one last year. Beside her, Robert dipped his straight pen into the ink and began to copy the notes on the chalkboard.

Jolene picked up her own pen. She ran her fingers across its hard nib and watched Robert. It didn't look that difficult to use. Carefully, she dipped the nib of the pen into the ink, extracted it and pulled it towards her page. Drops of midnight blue ink splashed onto her desktop. Quickly, she dabbed at the lakes with her fingers, turning them into small puddles. She wiped her stained fingers on her trousers and tried again, this time barely dipping the nib of the pen into the ink. Her pen reached the paper leaving behind a small stream of ink on the desktop. *Ner* she wrote in her best handwriting, watching the ink fade away with each letter. The pens were scratchy and difficult to write with. She inked her pen again, noticing that Robert was onto his second line. *vous.* Hurriedly, she dipped her pen again and added *ly.* The ink sloshed into a slough on her page. She turned her wrist to blot it, spraying a fine fountain of ink across the paper. Horrified, she covered her face, forgetting about the still-wet ink on her fingertips. Beside her, Robert suddenly burst into laughter.

Jolene saw Miss Trudell turn almost as if in slow motion. The teacher's eyes narrowed and instantaneously, all the eyes of the classroom turned towards Jolene's ink-smeared face. Miss Trudell loomed larger and larger as she made her way towards Jolene's desk, until she filled the aisle. Jolene closed her eyes and waited.

"Stand up!" demanded Miss Trudell.

Jolene jumped to her feet, banging the shelf below her desk and sending all of Samuel's things cascading to the floor.

"Do you always require so much attention?"

"No, never," said Jolene truthfully. "It's just that our school at home . . . " she glanced around nervously. "Well, it's a lot different is all." She tucked her soiled hands into the sleeves of her jacket.

"In this school, you will do things as instructed," barked Miss Trudell. Jolene nodded. "You can clean yourself up at lunch recess. Now pick up those things." Miss Trudell moved towards the front of the room, her skirt swishing across the floor. Jolene collected Samuel's books and scribblers and sank back into her desk.

"Very well," said Miss Trudell a few moments later. "Let's move on to the geography spelling bee. Boys line up on the right side of the room, girls on the left."

Carefully, without banging her desk, Jolene stood up and crossed the room to the left-hand side. She stood behind Edna, staring at her boots and waiting for instructions.

A low buzz went round the classroom and Jolene looked up to find Miss Trudell, her hands on her hips, standing in front of her. "Is this your idea of following instructions?"

Jolene looked around. Across the classroom, Daniel's hazel eyes were bright and his hands were motioning for her to join him. Of course, she was supposed to be a boy and she was standing in the girls' line. She couldn't suppress a giggle. It was all so ludicrous.

"So you think it's funny, do you?" said Miss Trudell in a high-pitched voice. "Perhaps you won't think this is so funny." She strode to the front of the room, opened the desk drawer and pulled out a long, leather strap. "Come here!" she demanded.

Silence fell on the class. Jolene could hear the thumping of her heart as she made her way towards the teacher's desk. "I'm sorry, Miss . . . "

"Silence!" commanded Miss Trudell. "Hold out your hands."

Jolene eyed the thick leather strap and swallowed hard. Beads of sweat trickled from her forehead into her eyes. She took a deep breath and held out her ink-stained hands, palms up.

Nobody breathed as Miss Trudell raised the strap. Then suddenly, a knock sounded at the door and a young girl burst in. "Miss Trudell," she said in an out-of-breath voice. "Mr. Horne sent me. The inspector's here."

Miss Trudell let the strap fall in a listless arc. She swung instantly about to face the messenger. "Who is it?"

"Monsieur Dupont."

A smile spread over the teacher's face. "Put these books away immediately and take out your French scribblers. Quickly, there's no time to waste. Daniel, take Jo outside and get him cleaned up. Robert, wipe up that desk." She returned the strap to her desk drawer, smoothed down the front of her skirt and launched into a French folksong, her hands clapping invitingly.

Daniel and Jolene half-ran, half-walked to the door.

Jolene's legs trembled as they took the steps two at a time until they reached the exit door and burst into the school-yard. Daniel scrutinized her, shaking his head. "You sure do act odd," he began.

Jolene looked down at her ink-smeared trousers and her stained fingers. "Where's the water?" she asked, ignoring his remarks.

Daniel led her over to a rain barrel. She dipped her hands into the barrel and splashed the cold water over her face. She dug out the hanky Grandpa had given her earlier and watched the ink spread in misshapen butterflies on the cloth. "Who's the inspector?" she asked, wiping the last of the ink from her face.

"Oh, he comes once a year to see if the teacher's teaching and we're learning like we're supposed to."

Jolene frowned. "And are we?"

"I think so, although there's so many other things I'd like to know. Still, I think Miss Trudell's a pretty good teacher."

Jolene wasn't so sure. How could anyone learn anything with a teacher with a temper like Miss Trudell's and those ridiculous pens?

Daniel turned towards the doors. "We'd better go in before the inspector gets there. He's a French man and Miss Trudell speaks fluent French. Mine's pretty good. How's yours?"

"*Très bien*," replied Jolene. At least French was one thing she did know, having gone to a French immersion school for six years. "*Très, très bien.*"

And it was, although Miss Trudell cringed when the inspector, having interrupted a studious French class conjugating verbs, took over and posed the first French question to Jolene. *"D'où viens-tu?"* he asked.

Where did she come from? For a split second, she thought of telling him that she was from Calgary, from the future. But she did not want to even imagine his or Miss Trudell's reaction to that kind of response. *"Je viens de Calgary,"* she said with an accent that rivalled Miss Trudell's.

The inspector's bushy eyebrows arched. He paused, his fingers intertwined behind his back. *"Et que penses-tu de cette région?"*

Jolene stole a look at her classmates. Edna's eyes were wide with wonder, Robert obviously was not following a word of their conversation and even Daniel seemed impressed. Only Miss Trudell seemed to understand their discussion. *"C'est une belle région,"* she began, choosing her words carefully. *"J'adore les grandes montagnes, les rivières brillantes et comment les arbres couvrent les collines."* She had, she realized, told the truth. She did love the mountains, the sparkling rivers and the way the trees covered the hills. It was beautiful here.

Monsieur Dupont smiled approvingly at Miss Trudell, who beamed at Jolene. *"Et ton père, il va travailler dans la mine?"*

"Non!" The word was out of her mouth before she had time to think. No, Grandpa was not going to work in the mine here. She took a deep breath to calm the emotions

that had surprised her. The inspector had tilted the woolen shoulders of his suit and was regarding her curiously through his wire-rimmed glasses. "*Non,*" she repeated, more softly this time. She did not want Grandpa to work underground, in the dark heart of Turtle Mountain. "*Probablement, il va chercher quelque chose dans le village.*" She knew he had no intention of working, in town or elsewhere, but she could hardly tell this prim man that Grandpa was a storyteller by trade.

The inspector nodded, his jaw angling back and forth beneath sharp cheekbones. "*Bon!*" he said ending the conversation and walking towards Miss Trudell. "You appear to be doing an excellent job," he told her before exiting briskly into the corridor.

The class murmured. Edna stared wide-eyed at Jolene, awe in her eyes. The echo of footsteps died in the corridor. Jolene blushed and looked down at her desk, its top still faintly polluted with ink.

"Well," said Miss Trudell, smiling broadly. "You were all very well behaved." She nodded in Jolene's direction. "You especially, Jo." Jolene nodded in return, thankful to have redeemed herself in some small way. "Now, I do believe that it is time for lunch." Miss Trudell picked up her school bell and rang it.

Chapter Ten

The students collected their lunchboxes and ran down the steps to the schoolyard. "Here," said Daniel, offering Jolene half a sandwich and a carrot. "Don't expect your grandpa had time to pack a lunch for you, but Ma gave me plenty."

Jolene murmured her thanks, her stomach doing the same. She sank down alongside the rough stone of the schoolhouse and chewed thoughtfully. She'd just lived through the most embarrassing morning of her life and she'd almost been strapped by a teacher. She exhaled, a long, steady breath in the warmth of the spring breeze and bit off the end of her carrot. And she'd survived. In fact, it hadn't been all that bad. Maybe Grandpa was right. Maybe there were worse things than looking like a fool.

Robert ran by them, pulled Edna's curls and bolted around the corner of the schoolhouse. A group of girls assembled around Edna, buzzing excitedly. Jolene shook her head. Some things didn't change, no matter the time.

"Want to play baseball?" asked Daniel. He stuffed the remainder of his lunch in his mouth and stood up.

"Sure!" Jolene said jumping to her feet and pulling on her cap. A few slivers of snow remained in the cool shadows, but the ground was firm and only muddy in a few spots.

Edna removed herself from the group of giggling girls and approached them. "You sure speak good French, Jo," she said, inclining her head to one side and letting her blond curls cascade around her shoulders.

"Thanks," muttered Jolene. She could feel her fingers tingle with embarrassment. Beside her, the boys snickered and Daniel backed away.

"Would you like a cookie, Jo?" asked Edna, moving towards her.

Jolene could feel the colour creep up her throat and into her cheeks. "No, no thanks," she mumbled, stumbling backwards towards Daniel.

Edna extended a hand, her creamy palm turned upwards to reveal an oatmeal cookie. "They're very good. I made them myself."

Jolene took a few unsteady steps backwards as the boys burst into laughter, then bolted around the back of the schoolhouse. Without hesitation, she turned and ran.

A sandy haired boy with freckles was already in the midst of the ball players, imitating Edna. "Would you like a cookie, Jo?" he mimicked as Jolene joined them looking as though she had just made a narrow escape. "I made them myself, especially for you." The others erupted in laughter and Jolene joined in. Only Robert said nothing.

They divided into teams and started a game of scrub. Robert was on the pitcher's mound when Jolene took her turn at bat. He threw a hard fastball. She swung and missed. "Hey, not so hard," said the catcher, a small boy named Graham.

Jolene turned back towards Robert. The pitch had been a hard one, the hardest he'd thrown all game. "What's the matter, too fast for you, Jo?" Robert taunted. He looked towards the sidelines where a few of the girls, including Edna, stood watching.

So that was what this was all about! It was all so crazy — Robert liking Edna, Edna liking her, her being a girl and yes, she admitted, liking Robert. She tried to concentrate on the things that Grandpa had taught her over the years — shoulders back, elbow high, wrists cocked. Robert wound up and pitched. Again, she swung, feeling the bat wrap around her. The ball slapped into the catcher's hands.

Jolene chewed on her bottom lip. As the next pitch crossed the cap that served as home plate, she straightened up and let it go by. Robert pursed his lips, said nothing and pitched again. Jolene swung. She heard the bat connect with a soft crack. The ball leapt upwards and flew backwards above the catcher's head. A foul ball! They all turned to watch as it narrowly missed a windowpane and landed on the second-storey ledge of the schoolhouse, settling into a crevice near the corner.

"Well done," said Robert sarcastically as Jolene wished she could disappear into the present.

The boys surveyed the situation. "Gee willikers," said Graham. "It's not even close to a window."

It was true. The nearest window was about four metres away from the ball. "We'll have to see if there's a ladder in the basement," said Robert. He looked deliberately at Jolene. "You coming with me?"

Jolene blushed and Daniel stepped to her side. "No," he said decisively.

"Why not?" whispered Jolene.

"It's creepy," muttered Daniel, under his breath.

"Scared?" taunted Robert, drawing out the vowel. His eyes glinted like waves in the sun.

"I'm not scared," said Jolene matter-of-factly, tugging at her sleeves.

"Of course he's not scared," said Daniel quickly. "He doesn't need to go."

"Oh, and how's he gonna' go about getting the ball back then?" A storm was brewing in Robert's eyes.

Daniel's voice was quiet and confident. "Jo can walk that ledge."

Jolene's head snapped up. Daniel's eyes met hers; they gleamed with pride. "That ledge is no problem for Jo," he said again. He turned and stared defiantly at Robert.

Jolene gulped. With her eyes, she traced the path from the window to the ball. It was at least four metres and the ledge that encircled the building looked pretty narrow.

Robert studied her skeptically. The rest of the boys stayed silent. "So let's see you do it," he said finally.

A few minutes later, Daniel and Jolene stood inside a second-storey classroom, staring out the window. A large group of boys and girls had assembled below them. "Wouldn't it be better to go into the basement or get someone?" Jolene asked Daniel. She remembered their caretaker throwing dozens of balls off the school roof at home.

Daniel ignored her. "There's one bit where a chunk of the ledge has fallen away," he said pointing down the wall. "Be careful."

Jolene looked in the direction Daniel had indicated. The ledge was almost twice the width of the balance beam at home, but there was no wall bordering the beam. She might be able to curl her fingers into the stones, but otherwise there were no handholds. She hesitated. What if she fell? It wasn't all that far to the ground. She might not break anything, but she would certainly look like a fool. She looked back at Daniel, his jaw set, his eyes firm. He believed in her and suddenly that mattered more than anything. She bent down and took off her socks and boots.

"What are you doing?"

"I left my gymnastics slippers at home," she muttered, not bothering to explain. "Wish me luck."

She stepped through the window and rubbed the rough concrete with her toes. The ledge was too narrow to stand sideways on, and because it was slightly angled, creeping along the ledge with her belly to the wall was out of the question. She dug the fingers of her right hand between the stones and balanced on the balls of her feet. Below her, anxious eyes watched. There was only one way to do this. She would simply have to walk it, straight ahead, as if she were on a balance beam. She took a deep breath and blew out slowly. Her left foot swooped below the ledge and she placed it directly in front of her right one. That wasn't so bad. Moving her right foot, the one against the wall was going to be more difficult. She extended her left arm straight out and slid her right foot forward to her left heel. So far, so good. Swoop, slide, swoop, slide, swoop, slide. She swayed once, but clawed her fingers into the wall and held on with her bare toes. She was almost at the place where the ledge had broken away now and she stopped to study it.

A good portion of the ledge was gone, broken off, almost as if something hard had fallen from above it. Jolene figured that the gap must be the length of a long stride, and she wanted to step forward, over it, with her left foot. After that it was only two or three steps to reach the ball. She hesitated for a moment, but did not look down. Then she dipped her left foot and swung it forward. Her toe brushed the edge of the ledge on its way up and it crumbled. Jolene dug her fingers into the wall and pulled her weight backwards. Bits of concrete and dust cascaded to the ground. Below her, someone shrieked.

"You okay?" called Daniel's voice behind her.

Jolene's heart hammered in her head. She pushed her weight back onto her heels to stop her knees from trembling. Then, consciously breathing in deep breaths, she shook her fingers, feeling the knot in her shoulders loosen.

On the other side of the missing ledge, the concrete was cracked and covered with dust. She couldn't be sure that it had not been weakened or damaged like the part she'd just brushed her foot against. She did some quick calculations. She would have to step over the whole dust-covered area to be safe and it was probably close to a metre. Normally that would have been an easy leap, but now, clutching the schoolhouse wall on a crumbling ledge, Jolene wasn't so sure. She looked down at the faces below her. She could turn back, if she could turn around. She glanced at Daniel over her shoulder.

"I knew he couldn't do it," said Robert's voice beneath her.

"It's so dangerous," breathed a girl's voice that she recognized as Edna's.

Jolene looked down. Dozens of eyes stared at her; dozens of students held their breath. Every one of them would know if she turned back. She took a deep breath and thought about Michael. What would he do if he were in her situation? It was no help. He would never have been able to walk this ledge; he was scared of heights. She studied the upturned eyes below her. They would know, and so would she! Jolene made up her mind. Dipping her left foot below the ledge, she concentrated, then leaped over the gap with both feet. Behind her, Daniel gasped as she teetered precariously. She dug her toes into the concrete, clawed the wall with her fingers and bent her knees, hanging on with every muscle in her body. And then her balance returned. She walked the last two steps and, with her toes, flicked the ball off the ledge.

"Hurray!" screamed the voices below her, but they were interrupted by a high-pitched squeal. A small child had come around the corner and stood looking horrified at Jolene balanced on the ledge.

"I'm telling," he screamed and bolted for the doors of the school.

Jolene looked anxiously at Daniel. She had no doubt that she was breaking a rule and in this school in 1903, she could only imagine what a suitable punishment might be.

"Oh no, you don't." It was Robert's voice and in seconds he had caught the young snitch by the collar.

"Let go," screamed the boy.

Robert relaxed his grip, but did not release the child. "You have two choices. I can wrap you in my horse blanket until school's out or you can stand here and watch Jo walk back on that ledge."

The boy deliberated only for a second. "I'll watch," he said wisely.

And he did. Holding the corner of the schoolhouse, Jolene pivoted on one foot. Then she navigated her way back along the ledge, skipped over the missing piece and climbed safely through the window.

"I knew you could do it," said Daniel, slapping her on the shoulder. "You're a brave lad you are!"

Jolene felt the muscles in her body relax one by one as she gave in to her fatigue. She had been brave. A week ago, she'd have never taken that risk. She felt elated and tired. "What would have happened if that boy had told on me?" Jolene asked, pulling on her socks and boots.

Daniel rolled his eyes. "You'd have been strapped, I suppose. We'd have both been strapped."

Somehow Jolene wasn't surprised. She looked up at Daniel with a new respect before following him out of the building. Graham stood holding the baseball in the schoolyard, but there didn't appear to be much interest in continuing the game. Jolene crossed the yard to the rain barrel. She dipped her dusty hands in the cool water and rubbed them thoughtfully together.

"You're good." The voice washed over her in one enormous wave.

She glanced up at Robert. "Thanks." Her gaze travelled to the young boy who had threatened to tell on her. "Do you really have a horse blanket?"

Robert laughed. "I do. My horse is over there yonder." He

pointed towards a small chestnut mare tethered to a fence. Three other horses stood alongside her.

"You ride to school?"

"Every day. I live on a ranch just past the railway camp."

Jolene knew the place. It was close to the time crease. She looked down at her borrowed outfit. Maybe these were Robert's clothes she was wearing.

"Where'd you come from?"

"Calgary." She smiled at Robert. "And you? Are you Canadian?"

"No, I'm from Newfoundland," he said, stressing the final syllable.

Jolene glanced up confused. Newfoundland was part of Canada. But it hadn't joined confederation until 1949, she recalled. Robert ambled in the direction of his horse and Jolene fell into step beside him. His shoulder brushed hers, but she did not pull away, relishing his nearness, wishing that each step would stand still in time.

"Did you come for the mines?" he asked, breaking the silence.

"Not really, and you?"

"No, father loves the wide open spaces. First the sea, now the ranch."

"Will you go back to the sea?" Her question was soft like the waves of his voice.

"I will," he said with great certainty. "I love the sea."

The bell rang and they made their way to the schoolhouse. Robert held the door open for Edna who passed by him with a smile. Jolene climbed the steps beside him. She followed Robert's gaze to Edna's sun-drenched hair bouncing just a few steps in front of her. "I prefer brunettes," she whispered truthfully.

The afternoon passed quickly, with, much to Jolene's relief, very little writing. Math was an easy affair, and except for once when she had to bite her tongue and respond in feet rather than metres, she fared well. Beside her, Robert squirmed restlessly. The day must be almost over.

"And just before you leave, a quick hygiene test." Miss Trudell passed out the hygiene scribblers.

Jolene fingered hers nervously as her young teacher posed the questions. "Number one: How often should you bathe in order to ensure proper cleanliness?"

Jolene studied her paper. She never bathed, but she showered five times weekly after gymnastics. Still in 1903, they probably didn't bath as often. She wrote 3 times a week on her paper, but only the number was legible.

"Number two: Describe a proper dental program to maintain healthy teeth."

Did they have dental floss in 1903? Jolene pictured her own mint-flavored floss, then decided against it. Brush 3 times daily and visit your dentist twice a year she wrote almost illegibly in ink blobs.

"Question number three: What bone structure protects your heart and lungs?"

At least she knew this one. *Rib cage*. She was finally starting to get the hang of the pens.

Miss Trudell circled the room. Jolene bent over her answers, blotted and dotted with ink. "Why is it important to wash your hair every week?"

Every week? Jolene stared at Miss Trudell's auburn hair piled into a bun high on her head. She washed hers every time she showered. Beside her, Robert's pen ran fluidly across the page. Surely she couldn't just say that it was important to keep it clean. The ink dripped from her pen.

"And finally," continued Miss Trudell, "describe one common method of helping heal the common cold."

Jolene glanced sideways at Daniel. Time was running out and she'd already left the previous question unanswered. *Echinacea tablets* she scrawled, picturing Miss Trudell's puzzled expression as she marked her answers.

"Okay, you may leave your scribblers open. For homework tonight, I want you to think about what life will be like in the future. What will our world be like in a century, in 2003? You may collect your things."

And then, it was over, the bell in Miss Trudell's hand clanging loudly.

They filed out the doors of the school together — Daniel, Robert, Edna and herself. "I bet there will be dozens of horseless carriages in a century's time. Everyone will have one," said Edna.

"In a hundred years," said Daniel, "the mines will be safe, clean places to work."

"And Frank will be a huge city with a great hockey team," added Robert. He looked sideways at Jolene. "What do you think it will be like?"

Jolene shivered. "In a hundred years," she said softly, gazing up at Turtle Mountain, "things will be very different."

Chapter Eleven

After Edna and Robert had left, Daniel took a gulp of fresh air and pointed to the hills north of the valley. "Want to go exploring?" he asked.

"Daniel, there you are," said a girl's voice behind them. They spun around to face a thin girl about eleven or twelve years old waving a package in the air. Bluish-grey eyes flitted above delicate cheekbones. Her long hair, secured with a scrap of material, hung braided down her back. "Ma wants you to take this out to Mrs. O'Neill. She's been ill." She handed Daniel the parcel and watched the disappointment flood his face.

"But that's so far," he groaned.

"It is not," retorted the girl, who Jolene surmised must be Daniel's sister. "And Ma said to make sure you know that the coal lamps need refilling."

Daniel groaned again. He swung the parcel in one listless arm. "Can't you take it, Elizabeth? Jo and I had plans."

Elizabeth glanced sideways at Jo. "No, I can't. I've got to go to work." She turned and strode away.

"Your sister?" asked Jolene, watching the steady bounce of the girl's braid.

"Mmm," murmured Daniel. "That's a stroke of bad luck." He glanced impatiently at the hills. "Want to come with me to Mrs. O'Neill's?"

Jolene shrugged. "Sure," she said watching Elizabeth turn down a side street. "Doesn't your sister go to school?"

"No, she quit this year to work at the boarding house. It doesn't pay much, but everything helps."

No wonder Daniel was worried about having to quit school and go to work. His younger sister had already done so. "What does she do there?"

"Cleans and cooks mostly, I guess. There's a house full of hungry miners to feed and the landlady she works for is a real stickler for cleanliness."

"That reminds me," said Jolene. "How'd you do on the hygiene test?"

"Every year they ask us the same questions. As if we don't know that we should bath every Saturday and wash our hair to keep from getting lice."

Jolene squirmed. She hadn't even thought of lice, although she had heard of some schools having it. "And how often do you see the dentist?"

Daniel looked puzzled. "I ain't never seen the dentist yet. But Ma makes me brush once a day."

"And what did you put for the last one, the one about having a cold?"

Daniel kicked at a pebble. "Just the usual, goose grease on the chest."

"Goose grease?"

"Why?" asked Daniel, looking up. "Did you put garlic and onions?"

"Not exactly," admitted Jolene, grinning. They walked in silence, their boots leaving telltale tracks in the dirt.

Daniel sniffed the package. "Butter," he said inhaling deeply, "and probably some jam."

"Why is your mother sending her butter and jam?"

"Everyone does. She's a widow, her health's poor and she's got no children. Nobody can afford the time or money to look after her completely, so they all do a little bit. Ma calls it the good neighbour system."

It was such a simple answer, such a simple idea and yet somehow over the years, things had changed. Jolene wondered what Grandpa was doing. "I don't ever want to get old," she said suddenly.

Daniel regarded her curiously. "Yeah," he agreed. "Pa always says that we're a short time living and a long time dead."

In her mind, Jolene saw the photograph of the buried cottages. She glanced at Turtle Mountain, wondering if she should tell Daniel, try to warn him somehow. Grandpa had told her that she couldn't change history, but she hadn't yet tried. Discreetly, she studied Daniel's eyes. If she told him, would he even believe her?

They had reached Dominion Avenue and their boots clip-clopped down the boardwalk. Daniel pointed to a group of men gathered in front of a shop. A bright red and white pole swirled above them. BARBER SHOP read the sign. "Come on, let's go see what's happening." Jolene followed him across the street.

The men's voices reached her ear. "So this is it, Elio — your last night as a bachelor. What will you do?"

A young man in his late twenties shrugged and smoothed his hair back around his ears. Jolene could see that it was newly cut.

"If ya knew what was good for ya, ya'd high tail it out of here. Grab the first good horse ya saw and leave."

The men laughed. "He's right!" drawled another one. "Women mean trouble, just ask me, I know."

"That's Mr. Brazeau," whispered Daniel, indicating the man who had just spoken. "He's got six daughters and a wife." He scrunched up his nose in disgust.

Jolene bit her tongue and made no comment.

"I don't know," began a musical voice. "I've seen a picture of Elio's bride-to-be. Don't know if I'd be in such a hurry to run off. All these guys, they're just hoping you'll get cold feet, so they can step in in your place, Elio."

"Sure hope she's as pretty as the picture," admitted Elio, blushing.

"Aye," agreed a Scottish accent. "I remember a lad I knew in Fort Macleod. Got this picture of his bride-to-be in a letter from her and was she a pretty lass. Young and fair, a real beauty. He could hardly contain himself, he could. Couldn't believe his good luck. But when he got to the station, she weren't there. He wandered 'round clutching her picture, searching for this fair-haired angel, thinking that maybe she hadn't gotten on the ship, that maybe something had gone wrong. Finally, he went up to this old woman, probably twenty years his senior and showed her the picture, asked her if she'd seen the young lass. And she looked at him and said, 'Aye, that's me, twenty years ago.'"

The men roared with laughter and Elio groaned. "Don't be telling stories like that, not today."

The singsong voice cut in again. "Don't despair Elio, lad. Or if you aim to, why not do it over a glass of whiskey?"

A loud cheer erupted and the group slowly manoeuvred its way across the street towards the Frank Hotel.

"What was that all about?" asked Jolene, watching them carry Elio over the dirt road and through the swinging doors of the hotel.

"His bride must be coming in on the passenger train."

"His bride?"

Daniel turned west. "Yeah, his bride."

"And he's never seen her?"

"He's got a picture."

"But he's never met her?"

Daniel shook his head. "He ordered her by mail."

"He ordered her by mail?" Jolene's voice echoed Daniel's words. People ordered flower seeds and CD's by mail. People didn't order brides by mail.

Daniel leaped off the boardwalk. "Yep," he said simply. "And she arrives tomorrow."

"But why?"

"Because that's when the Spokane Flyer, the passenger train, arrives." Daniel scowled at her.

Jolene stared blankly at him. "No, why would you order a bride by mail?"

Daniel was losing patience. "Well, there ain't many young women around here, except for Miss Trudell at school and a few others. Lots of the men order brides from Europe. That way they get someone who speaks the same language, cooks the same, you know."

"What about love?" The words were out of her mouth before she had even realized she'd spoken them.

"Love?" asked Daniel, scrunching up his nose again. "What's that got to do with it?"

"You know, first you fall in love, then you get married."

Daniel threw her a suspicious look, but said nothing. He picked up the pace and Jolene had to hurry to keep up with him. She thought fleetingly of Robert and Gerard. Not that she loved them exactly, but thinking of them did make her heart skip. But here, here it was different. Here, you worked hard, long hours in the house, on the ranch, in the mine. There didn't seem to be much time for play or love.

Around the corner, an enormous mountain rose, like an opaque dome in the sky. Jolene stopped in her tracks. "That's Crowsnest Mountain," said Daniel. "Nesting place of the crows."

Jolene spun about, looking back at Turtle Mountain, then up at Crowsnest Mountain and the seven small peaks that jutted up beside it. There was something majestic, yet frightening about being in the middle of these towering rocks, especially knowing that one night Turtle Mountain would come sliding down into this very valley. "Daniel," began Jolene, but the sound of a horse's hooves interrupted her.

They whirled about as a man on a chestnut mare pulled alongside them. "Daniel," he called, "where are you off to?"

"Taking a parcel to Mrs. O'Neill." Daniel held up the package.

The mounted rider laughed. "You and me, we're on the same mission." He indicated his saddlebag. "The missus had the same thought. I'll take that the rest of the way for you, if you like."

"Thanks," breathed Daniel, glad to be relieved of his chore. He held up the package and watched as the man tucked it into a saddlebag and continued on his way.

"Come on," called Daniel, sprinting back towards town.

"We've still got enough light to go exploring. Maybe we'll find the lost Lemon Mine."

Jolene raced along beside him. The wind had picked up and the heavily wooded hills looked dark and sinister. Thoughts of bears filled her mind.

Daniel jumped up onto the boardwalk and began to run, full out.

"Daniel MacEachern!" A stern voice reached out from a doorway and grabbed him. Daniel reeled to a stop. Jolene crashed into him from behind. "And just where do you think you're going, galloping down the boardwalk like a couple of hooligans?" Daniel's mouth gaped, but he made no sound. The stout woman in front of him hardly seemed to notice. "First, running about like this in town here, and then . . . mark my word, you'll be running into trouble, Daniel."

She narrowed her eyes at Jolene. Her lips pursed themselves into a wrinkled frown. "And who might this be?" Again, Daniel's mouth flapped, but no words managed to escape. "I haven't seen you at church, lad," she said, addressing Jolene. She pounded a finger on the book that had, up to now, been tucked beneath her arm. Jolene could read the glittering gold letters: Holy Bible. "You tell your folks that they're right welcome, expected in fact, at the Presbyterian Church this Sunday, ten o'clock sharp."

"That they are, welcome that is," said a kind voice behind them. Jolene turned to see a small man with an incredibly large moustache shaped like the handlebars of her mother's old bicycle.

"Hiya Reverend," said Daniel, smiling.

"Daniel." The small man grinned beneath his moustache. "Mrs. Bailey," he said, nodding in the direction of the stout woman who smoothed her dress over her ample hips. "And where are you two lads off to then?" asked the minister.

"Just up in the hills to do a bit of exploring," said Daniel.

"My word!" exclaimed Mrs. Bailey. She rolled her eyes dramatically. "In the hills yet."

The minister glanced up the valley wall. "Be careful, Daniel. There were two bears sighted up there this past week. It might not be a good idea to go now. It'll be dark soon."

"We'll be careful," said Daniel as he and Jolene continued down the boardwalk.

They walked in silence, Jolene's mind filled with memories of her bear encounter. Was it really a smart thing to do, to go up into the hills at dusk? Jolene glanced down at her borrowed clothes. Being a boy did make her feel braver, but she wasn't sure if hiking in bear country after dark was courageous or just plain stupid. "The Reverend's right," she said tentatively. "It'd be better to go in the daylight."

"You ain't scared, are you?"

Jolene took a deep breath. "Yes," she admitted. "I am."

Daniel stopped walking. He studied her curiously.

"Aren't you?" she asked.

Daniel looked down at his boots. For a long moment, he said nothing. Then, abruptly, he looked her square in the eyes. "I guess you're right," he admitted. "We ought not to go."

Jolene breathed a sigh of relief. She felt, somehow, as if she'd been as brave now as she had been on the ledge at school.

"Besides," said Daniel, "while we're here I may as well show you one of my secret spots."

He turned down a dirt path until he reached the dense brush behind a row of houses. Daniel crashed through it with Jolene following closely behind. Soon they came upon a grassy clearing, completely canopied by overhanging branches. A young woman dressed in a navy skirt was walking in circles, her arms extended to the side beneath her white shawl.

"Isn't that Peggy?" whispered Jolene.

"Crazy Peggy," answered Daniel. He stepped into the clearing.

Peggy turned to face them at once. Her eyes were bright, alive and incredibly green. "They flew! Big metal birds with long wings, all lit up like stars. Up in the sky they were, roaring like thunder. It's a small miracle, Daniel, a small miracle." Her voice was breathless with excitement.

"It's okay, Peggy," said Daniel in a soothing voice. "Why don't you let us take you home?"

Peggy shook her head. She scratched at a mole on the

back of her left hand, then spread her arms wide again. "I saw them, Daniel, I saw them. Huge silver birds swooshing through the clouds, back and forth across the hills as if they were looking for something."

Planes flying search and rescue, thought Jolene.

"Of course you did," said Daniel to Peggy. "Now let's go home and tell your mother." He took her gently by the elbow and steered her down the path.

"I must tell father," Peggy said quickly. "He must know at once."

Walking behind them, Jolene listened to Peggy describe what she had seen. Had she gone through a time crease, but rather than going into the past, gone into the future? Jolene's mind raced. Could she and Grandpa do the same? If only she could find a way to talk to Peggy alone, or perhaps to Peggy's father.

But she didn't have the chance. Peggy's mother thanked them both, and with an anxious look, whisked her daughter inside. Jolene lingered behind, but there was no point waiting around. Peggy had been locked securely inside her little white house covered in a thin layer of coal dust.

The mountain's shadow had cast the town in a grim greyness. "There's a ball practice at the recreation field. Let's go on over that way," suggested Daniel.

When they were safely down the road, Jolene asked, "What will happen to Peggy?"

Daniel shrugged. "There's not much you can do when

people lose their minds, is there? Maybe they'll send her away or lock her in." He broke into a trot, as if he could out-run the uncomfortable thought.

Would that happen to Grandpa if Mom and Dad really believed that he was losing his mind? Jolene ran to catch up with Daniel, leaving her own thoughts behind.

In the distance, they saw the men assembling on the ball field and picked up the pace. Jo was anxious to see Grandpa again. He was there twisting from the waist up, a bat across the back of his shoulders. "Hey Jo, how was school?" he called across the field.

Jolene moved close to him. "Next time we come, remind me to bring a real pen, will you?"

Grandpa laughed.

"I met your aunt," whispered Jolene.

"And?"

"I think she's found a way to go into the future."

Grandpa arched his eyebrows. "You'll have to tell me all your stories."

"That's a switch," said Jolene. Grandpa was the story-teller. She rarely told stories and neither did her friends — not like Old Man Warner. "Why don't people in the present tell as many stories anymore?"

"Too many distractions, so many other things to do, I suppose."

Jolene thought about their family room at home — the television, the stereo, the computer and internet, the video games. Yet there was something about hearing a great story, watching a fine storyteller. "Won't we lose those stories from the past?"

"Perhaps," said Grandpa. He brushed her cheek with his fingers. "You're starting to sound like your father."

A voice called and Grandpa crossed the field, leaving Jolene standing motionless, stunned by his words.

Chapter Twelve

A shrill whistle cut the air and Daniel jumped up from his spot on the bench where he and Jolene were sitting watching the ball practice. "Come on," he called. "If we hurry, we can catch Henry at the mine."

"Who's Henry?"

"My older brother." They arrived at the mine entrance just as the first miners stepped out of the gangway. A heavy, greasy stench filled the air. Jolene stared at the coal-covered miners. Would Daniel soon be one of them? Would he soon take his place in the thick darkness of the mine?

"That's the tipple," said Daniel, pointing to a brick building nearby. "Where they pick the rocks out of the coal. I guess that's where I'll be next year." His mouth swept downward in despair.

"You have to tell your parents that you want to be a lawyer, I mean a barrister, Daniel."

Daniel shrugged. "It won't make no difference. Pa would still want me to leave school and go mining."

"Could your mom convince him to let you stay?"

"Maybe, but how am I going to convince my mom?"

Jolene smothered a laugh. They lived a century apart, but they both had similar problems — how to convince their mothers and fathers.

"There he is!" Daniel raced towards a young man holding a water can and a lunchbox. His sweaty face was streaked with black and his clothes blanketed with fine black dust.

"Whoa!" the young man cried, holding up his arms. "Ma will have my head if you get covered in coal dust."

Jolene looked at the tired, filthy faces around her. "Why don't they use the washhouse?" she asked, glancing around for a long building that resembled the one Karen had shown her above the Bellevue mine.

Daniel stared blankly at her. "The what?"

Jolene blushed. "Never mind," she muttered more to herself than anyone else as they followed Henry.

"This is Jo," announced Daniel. "He and his grandpa just came into town. You oughta' see his grandpa play baseball!"

Henry smiled at Jolene. "Is that right? Well, I expect he'll be right welcome in this town then. You aimin' to stay here under Turtle Mountain?"

Jolene shrugged. "Why do they call it that?" She looked

up at the limestone ledge dividing the front face into horizontal layers.

"Guess they thought it was shaped like a turtle."

"That's part of it, Daniel," admitted Henry. "But the Blackfeet call it 'the mountain that walks'. They say it moves ever so slow, like a turtle, and none would ever camp at its base."

Daniel laughed aloud, but Jolene shivered. This very spot they were standing on would be buried by the slide. These people might be buried alive beneath the limestone boulders. Jolene felt her neck and shoulders grow tight. She caught Daniel's arm. "Daniel, the Blackfeet are right. The mountain is going to slide."

Henry chuckled.

"Really!" she insisted. "That whole part above the ledge is going to break off and slide down. This part of the town will be covered by ninety million tons of rock." Jolene looked desperately at Daniel and his brother.

Henry's face erupted in laughter. Daniel joined in, slapping her on the back. "You sure got some strange ideas," he said.

"This mountain's been around for more years than even the Blackfeet," said Henry, smiling kindly. "You don't have to worry about it moving, young Jo."

Jolene fell into step beside them. These kind people were living in the path of disaster. She had to find a way to warn them, to save them. "What's the date today?" she blurted out without warning.

Henry frowned in thought. "Not sure. The days run into the nights when you work underground. Must be the last week of April, I'd guess. Why?"

Before Jolene could answer, a cry went up in the distance and a horse galloped towards them. Daniel let out a shout. "Look, it's Old Charlie!" The same predictable horse she had seen on her first visit to Frank was galloping down the road towards the mine. Daniel cut the horse off and Old Charlie backed away in a circle, prancing nervously. Daniel lunged for the bridle and caught it between his fingers.

"He must be going to work," explained Henry. "Charlie pulls the coal cars, and usually, he's so . . . "

"Predictable," concluded Jolene.

Henry smiled quizzically at her. "Yes, predictable."

Karl had arrived and now held Old Charlie's lead rope. "Don't know what's got into him tonight. All of them, spooked or something."

Jolene stopped in her tracks. An ominous feeling settled over her and the wind gusted eerily. "I'd better go and find my grandpa," she said.

"He'll be on the ball field with the men, Jo, and then they'll wander over to the hotel for a drink," Henry told her. "You just come on home and have some supper. Ma's got five of us children. One more ain't going to make any difference. She probably won't even notice."

Jolene walked silently beside Daniel and his brother.

Grandpa's words were true. She couldn't change history. She couldn't warn them; they didn't believe her. But what about Grandpa and her? What would happen if they got stuck in the past and were crushed by the slide? They weren't a real part of 1903. But if they were killed, how would they ever get back to the present? Panic rose within her. What had Henry said? That it was the last week of April, and Old Man Warner had mentioned that it was almost May. Turtle Mountain had slid on April 29th, on a cold day after a few warm days. She inhaled the warm breeze and breathed a sigh of relief. It was too warm for the water in the cracks of the mountain to freeze tonight.

Jolene had been going to say her goodbyes when they reached the house and go find Grandpa. But the smell of supper and warm bread made her mouth water. She followed Daniel into the small, wooden cottage. In the centre of the largest room was a coal-burning stove. A kettle whistled on the stovetop and Daniel's mother stirred something in a large pot. A girl, about nine years of age, was setting the table. A toddler ran towards Daniel, tripped and fell onto the wooden floor. "Hey Peter," sang Daniel. He scooped the little boy up and bounced him on a bed near the wall.

Bit by bit, Jolene's eyes adjusted to the light of the coal-oil lantern on the table. A washtub and board stood in one corner. On a nail behind the stove hung a large tin tub — the bathtub, Jolene imagined, used only on Saturdays. Beds covered with feather quilts stood against the plastered walls.

Jolene thought guiltily of her own room at home with her flowered duvet, pine dresser and full-length mirror.

"Wash up, Daniel," called his mother over her shoulder. "And your friend as well."

Jolene followed Daniel to a washstand in the corner. He poured some water into the basin and she washed her hands and face.

"Aren't you going to introduce us?" asked Daniel's mother.

"This is Jo," answered Henry coming in from the porch. He had washed and changed out of his work clothes. "His grandpa's just arrived and I hear he's quite the ball player."

Ma sighed. "Trust your pa to find another ball player. I think that man loves baseball more than me." Henry laughed and gave his mother a hug. Ma plunked Peter into a chair. "How was working in the mine?"

"The bosses are after us to take the coal off the pillars. I don't know. Some say there'll be a heavy price to pay for robbing the coal seam. Still, it's easy money."

"Well you just be careful," ordered Ma fussing about the stove. She put a pot on the hot stove. "I can't figure these eggs," she said. "In Scotland, I could cook a soft-boiled egg just so. But here, I never seem to get them right. At first I thought that the brown ones took longer to cook, but now I'm not so sure. Poor Peter."

Jolene looked over Ma's shoulder. "It doesn't have any-thing to do with the eggs," she explained gently. "It's be-cause you're at a higher altitude here, and water boils at a lower temperature at higher elevations. That means that it would take longer to cook an egg here."

Ma looked at Jolene, surprise registering in her eyes. "Well I'll be. Fancy that." She paused. "Where'd you learn that anyway?"

"At school," said Jolene honestly.

The children slid onto the rough wooden benches around the table. "Sit down, lad," said Ma, gesturing towards Jolene. "There's plenty for everyone."

"Thank you." Jolene's voice was a soft whisper. She eased herself onto the bench next to Daniel. The children stared at her.

"Your cap," whispered Daniel. Jolene quickly pulled off her cap and tucked it into her pocket, thankful for the dim light of the lamp.

"Bless us, Lord," began Ma. "Watch over our men in the mine, protect each of these children and we ask a special blessing on our guest tonight. Amen."

"Amen," chorused the children. Ma ladled stew onto Jolene's plate and Daniel passed her a board with freshly cut bread. Jolene dug in. The stew was delicious, and the gravy was smooth and rich. She ate quietly, answering the questions she was asked and thinking.

After supper, Henry went out with some friends and Jolene helped Daniel clean and refill the lanterns. By the time they were done, they were covered in streaks as black as the night air. Jolene stood listening to the silence of the starry sky.

"I love the planets and constellations," whispered Daniel, joining her. "Pa knows all about them."

"We studied them last year," said Jolene. She stood looking upwards, recalling the night she had seen Mars out her bedroom window. "I don't see why all the planets are named after powerful gods rather than goddesses."

"There's Venus," offered Daniel.

"The goddess of love," recalled Jolene. "She was hardly a brave, strong figure."

"But she was!" exclaimed Daniel. "To the Greeks, she was Aphrodite, the great protectress during the Trojan War. That's why the Romans honoured Venus as the protectress of Rome."

Jolene regarded him curiously. "You mean she was a brave warrior?"

"Absolutely!"

Jolene drew her tongue along the enamel of her teeth. "I guess it just shows that we girls have as much reason to be as brave as you do," she said slowly and purposefully.

"We girls?" Daniel's voice cracked the stillness of the night.

"It's a long story, Daniel, but I'm actually a girl."

"A . . . what, you're a . . ." His voice died suddenly.

"I'm a girl. My name's Jolene." She could feel the confusion in his silence.

"Then why did you . . . ?"

"There you are," said Ma, coming out to fetch the last of the washing and interrupting Daniel's question. "You'd best wash up and get to bed." She rubbed the joints of her fingers. "Feels like the weather's going to change."

Inside, Daniel's youngest sister, Margaret, was busy giving Peter a bedtime snack. He played with the carrot she cut for him, bouncing on the bench at the same time. Jolene and Daniel gathered around the coal lantern. The flame mesmerized Jolene, but she could feel Daniel's questioning gaze on her. She smiled in his direction. Suddenly, Peter coughed and gagged. Ma rose immediately as her young son struggled to breathe. His face was red and distorted. His little shoulders heaved. Ma slapped him on the back, gently at first and then harder and harder as Peter's lips began to turn blue. Ma shot a desperate look at Daniel. Peter gurgled and Jolene leaped to her feet. The Heimlich manoeuvre! She'd learned it at school, but she'd never used it before. Peter's face was very blue by the time she reached him, but she didn't hesitate. She stepped in front of Ma, reached around Peter's almost-limp body, placed her fist at the base of his rib cage and with her other hand on top of it, gave a sharp pull, twisting her fist upwards at the same time. Peter coughed and sputtered. A chunk of carrot burst from his mouth and his little body lay draped across the table. Within moments, he had started to cry, a soft cry that filled the house and allowed the others to draw breath.

Ma hugged Peter to her as the colour crept back into his

face. Then she turned to Jolene and embraced her. "What can I say, child? You've quite possibly saved the life of my wee one. How I don't know, but I thank you just the same."

Daniel patted Jolene's shoulder, then stopped abruptly as if he had just remembered she was a girl.

"I learned that in school," said Jolene. "They teach us lots of useful things in school."

"I see that," said Ma.

"I want to be doctor," said Jolene purposefully.

"That's a worthy ambition," said Ma. "And what do your folks think of that?"

"They think it's a great idea. I'll have to stay in school for a long time, but it's worth it because then I'll be able to help many people." She paused. "Just like Daniel will be able to if he becomes a barrister."

Beside her, she could feel Daniel's body tense. The house fell silent. Even Peter's sobs subsided.

Ma looked from Jolene to Daniel. "You want to be a barrister?"

Daniel hesitated. "Yes," he said finally.

"To help the union negotiate for the miners," added Jolene.

She opened her mouth to continue, but Daniel's voice interrupted her. "But it would be expensive, Ma. I'd have to stay in school for many years and go on to study law after that."

Ma studied Daniel. "Well," she began, "you've always been a good student. You can work the summer months to earn a bit of money and the rest we'll find for you if we can."

Daniel lunged past Jolene, threw his arms around his mother's waist and hugged her. Ma laughed. She handed Peter, now calm but tired, to Margaret and bid her get him ready for bed. "How would one of you lads like to read from the Good Book?" asked Ma as she bustled about.

Daniel grimaced but picked up the Bible. "May I?" asked Jolene, taking it from him. She settled herself beside the lamp, chose the parable of the three servants and began to read. Her voice was soft but clear and the cottage listened silently as she read about how everyone must use the talents and gifts they are given and how that often means taking risks. By the time she had finished, the little ones were asleep.

"You have the voice of an angel," said Ma when Jolene was done. "That was just lovely, lad. Thank you."

"You're welcome." Jolene stood up and yawned. She hated to leave the warmth of the cottage, but she was beginning to worry about Grandpa. "I guess I should go and find my grandpa," she said.

"You'll do nothing of the sort," said Ma. She turned back a quilt on one of the beds near the stove. "Margaret's put the wee one down in our bed. He usually ends up there anyway. There's plenty of room." She patted the pillow. "Your grandfather will come on back here looking for you, so just sit yourself down and stay warm."

Jolene chewed her bottom lip nervously. Daniel's mom

was right. Grandpa would come back looking for her. And where would she even begin looking for him in the dark? She sat down gingerly on the edge of the bed. "If you don't mind, I'll just sit up and wait."

"Suit yourself," said Ma, busying herself near the stove. Jolene untied her boots, slid them off and backed up until her back was against the wall. She glanced towards Daniel who had already crawled into the bed next to hers.

"Goodnight, Daniel," she whispered into the darkness. She pulled the quilt around her feet.

"Goodnight, Jo." There was a long pause. "I mean, Jolene." There was another pause. "And thank you."

Jolene drew the covers up around her chin. The smell of warm yeast permeated the cottage and Ma fussed near the stove. The quiet of the night poured into the room and her eyelids grew heavy. Within minutes, she was asleep.

A hand laid her head gently on a pillow. "It's all right, young Jo," whispered a woman's voice. "Lie down now and stay warm. It's turned cold outside so I've just put some more coal on the stove."

"Where am I?" Jolene murmured, confused. "What day is it? What time?"

"You're here at Daniel's, lad," whispered the voice. "And it's round about four in the morning. I guess that would make it the 29th of April now. Go on back to sleep." A woman's face moved through the light of the lamp. "Go ahead now, sleep until morning." Her hand pushed Jolene gently down beneath the quilt. Her voice was soothing and comforting. Jolene snuggled under the covers as the lamp disappeared into the next room. Everything was fine, she told herself. She was in Daniel's house. And it was April 29th. She grinned sleepily. April 29, 1903.

"1903! April 29th!" Jolene sat up in bed. "Sometime around four in the morning." That was nearly the time of the slide! She leaped out of bed, shoved her feet into her boots and looked around the cottage. Bending low over Daniel's bed, she shook him. "Daniel, get up! The mountain's going to slide." Daniel rolled onto his back and murmured in his sleep. Jolene shook him harder, but he did not respond.

A horse whinnied in the distance and Jolene raced across the room towards the door. "Gramps!" she whispered. She had to find him. But how? He could be anywhere. Why hadn't he come for her? She pulled the door open and slipped outside, closing it firmly behind her. Her feet raced to the road. "Think, Jo, think!" she told herself. "Where would he be?" Then she was off, running as fast as her legs would carry her towards the stable. Karl had said there was a spare room there. She stumbled once and fell hard against the dirt. The air was heavy and hushed, ever so silent. She heard a horse whinny in the distance and ran across the wooden bridge in that direction. Grandpa had to be there!

Taking the steps two at a time, Jolene reached the top floor in seconds. A door opened on her left, another one on her right. She turned left and leaned against the wooden door. A thin beam of moonlight trickled into the room. A woolen jacket hung on the back of a chair. She crept quickly across the planks towards the bed. A man snored beneath a woolen blanket. A moustache twitched. "Gramps!" she whispered, shaking the blankets. "Gramps, it's Jo. Wake up!" Grandpa groaned in his sleep. She caught a stiff whiff of whiskey on his breath, then tugged at the blanket, pulling it completely off the bed. "Come on. We've got to get out of here." Grandpa moaned again and rolled over. "Get up!" ordered Jolene, as her grandfather's body rolled towards the edge of the bed.

Slowly, Grandpa opened his eyes. "Jo?" he asked.

"It's four in the morning on April 29th."

"April 29th?" he asked groggily.

"In 1903! The slide is going to come down. We've got to get out of here!"

Her voice was panicky now.

Grandpa leaned into the moonbeam and looked at his watch. "Goodness, Jo, you're right." He struggled to his feet and pulled on his shoes. "I meant to come find you last night after I'd had a few drinks with the baseball team. But Karl was there and I . . . "

"Never mind," called Jolene, urging him towards the door. Together they raced down the stairs and burst out into the night.

The air whispered and the mountain shrugged. Jolene

stopped and looked in the direction of the cottages. "Shouldn't we do something?" she gasped.

Grandpa shook his head. "No time, Jo, no time." She ran a few steps and stopped again. "Come on, Jo. It won't make any difference anyway."

Above them the mountain creaked softly.

Grandpa grabbed Jolene's arm. "Run! Now! As fast as you can."

Jolene needed no convincing. She ran, tears streaming down her face, her heart pulsing in her fingertips. They lost their way and circled blindly about until she found the railway tracks. "Over here!" she called. Grandpa ran towards Jolene's voice. "Stay on the tracks!"

Their feet pounded down the railway ties. Jolene concentrated on keeping her stride strong and even, so as not to trip. They were almost at the field near the time crease.

Behind her, she heard a heavy thud and a crash. She whirled around. Grandpa lay sprawled across the tracks. She raced back to him, dropping to her knees. "Gramps, are you okay?" Blood trickled from a cut on his forehead. He moaned softly. Jolene put an arm under his shoulders and shifted him until he was half-sitting. "Come on, Gramps, up," she urged. She had to get him on his feet, had to get him to the time crease. He murmured something incoherent and dabbed at the wound on his forehead. "Up," she repeated as he struggled to his feet. Above them, the mountain creaked again. It wasn't far, maybe a hundred metres.

She put her arm around his waist and wrapped his around her shoulders. "Lean on me," she breathed, staggering under his weight. They stumbled forward through the field.

He was breathing hard, drawing breath in great gulps. "Jo," he whispered, stopping. "You go. Go ahead without me. You're young. You still have . . . "

"No!" she said sharply. "Don't talk. Walk!"

His feet resumed their motion. They were in the crocus field now, his body leaning heavily against Jolene's.

"I can see the silhouette of the erratic. Straight ahead," she said, urging him on.

Grandpa's breathing grew heavier, more rapid.

Behind them, the mountain rumbled. Jolene looked back over her shoulder. Just a few more steps. Could she get them through the crease this time? She'd never done it before. Above them, there was a loud roar, like an almighty clap of thunder. An enormous slab of rock broke off and hurtled itself into the valley.

Jolene lurched forward into the dense shadow, pulling Grandpa with her. "One location in time," she whispered desperately, clenching her eyes shut. Something sharp sliced her shin and branches slapped her in the face. A blast of hot air hit Jolene. Behind them, dust choked the air and the ground trembled.

Jolene lifted her head and looked around. Her body lay draped across a moss-covered boulder. Beside her lay the crumpled body of her grandfather. "Gramps," she breathed. "Are you okay?"

Slowly, Grandpa lifted his head. The hair on his forehead was matted with blood. "Jo," he gasped. She flung her arms around his neck and wept. Her sobs filled the silence of the dawn. They accompanied the first rays of morning and orchestrated the rising of the sun. She cried until she could cry no more, her body giving in to a desperate sleep. For a long time, they lay motionless.

"It's all right, Jo, it's all right." In her sleep, Jolene heard her grandfather's voice. His hand touched her arm and she raised her head from his chest.

"Oh Gramps!" Jolene buried her face against his shoulder. "I was so afraid. I was so afraid that I wouldn't be able to get us back." She sat up and helped him do the same.

Grandpa's eyes met hers. "I never doubted you," he said softly. "You've always had that courage within you. You just didn't know it."

Jolene stared into her grandfather's eyes. Maybe he was right. She stood up and extended a hand to him. Slowly, stiffly, Grandpa struggled to his feet and leaned against her. Jolene turned and looked towards the jagged desert of rocks in the morning light. Her voice was a fragile whisper. "Did Daniel and his family...?"

Grandpa pulled her towards him. "Never mind that now, Jo. There will be time for knowing that later. Let's just go home."

Together they limped down the road. Occasionally, a tear rolled down Jolene's cheeks. Only once did she turn and look back over her shoulder, back at Frank Slide.

Chapter Thirteen

Grandpa was sitting on the edge of her bed when Jolene woke that afternoon. "I thought you were going to sleep forever."

Jolene adjusted her nightshirt and stretched. "What time is it?"

"Almost four o'clock. Your dad phoned to say he wouldn't be in until after supper."

Jolene swung her legs over the edge of the bed. Her shin throbbed, a sudden reminder of their near escape. "Last night — the slide. Turtle Mountain fell." She leaped to her feet. "We have to go back."

Grandpa rose stiffly. "I don't think that's such a good idea."

"But Daniel and his family. All those people, the miners

and . . ." Jolene stopped mid-sentence and leaned closer to her grandfather's face, lined and worn. She couldn't ever remember seeing him look so exhausted. "You went back while I was sleeping, didn't you?"

Grandpa's eyes focused on hers. "Yes, Jo."

"Why didn't you take me? I want to go back."

Granpa shuffled out of the bedroom into the living room and Jolene followed him. He stopped at the window and stood looking out at the slide, rocking back and forth in one spot. "Being able to go through the creases is exciting, Jo, but it's also dangerous. Those time creases are formed because there's lots of energy at that location and usually that energy comes from a celebration or a disaster." Grandpa sighed. "Seventy lives were lost, homes were wrecked and dreams were destroyed." He studied her face. "I can't stop you from going back now that you know how," he said gently, "but if you decide to go, I'd rather go with you." He gestured towards the boulders of the slide. "We see it now, one hundred years after the fact, but the morning after the mountain slid . . . It's pretty awful, Jo."

Jolene looked out at the sea of rocks. The stable and the railway construction camp, she knew, had been buried. So too, had Robert's ranch and his ocean-blue eyes. And the miners' cottages had all been destroyed. A lump rose in her throat, along with the realization that she really had no desire to return. "Gramps," she said finally, "Karen told us that some of those people in the cottages survived." She swallowed hard. "Daniel and his family — did they make it?"

Grandpa put an arm around her shoulders. "They did, Jo. By some miracle, they did."

Relief flooded over her. Again, she smelled Ma's rich stew, watched the colour come back into Peter's face and heard Daniel thank her in the evening stillness.

"Their house was ruined, but they were all okay — pinned beneath timbers, bruised and battered and absolutely terrified — but okay." Grandpa sighed. "If you'd seen their cottage all broken apart — well, it's amazing that they survived."

What would they do? Jolene thought about the butter and jam that Daniel's mother had sent for Mrs. O'Neill. People looked after people. Daniel and his family would start again with help. But would he, after all that, still be able to stay in school?

Jolene stood next to Grandpa for a long time, saying nothing, remembering. "I think I'll take a shower," she said finally, squeezing his arm.

Grandpa was sitting on the couch staring at the slide when she emerged, showered and dressed. He muttered something she couldn't understand and Jolene knew that, behind that dazed look, he was reliving the morning after the slide. Dad would be back soon and it wouldn't do to have Grandpa looking exhausted and not making sense. "Come on, Gramps. Why don't you lie down?" she said, pulling his arm gently until he was in a reclining position. Jolene brushed her hand across Grandpa's forehead. His eyes flickered and then closed as she watched anxiously.

Grandpa was dozing on the couch when Dad burst through the door and hustled into the dining room. Karen was right behind him. "Hi Jolene," he called. "I stopped to pick up some information at the interpretive centre and Karen was kind enough to join me." He patted his new lens. "We took some more photos. Just a few questions to ask Karen and then we can head home. Probably tomorrow."

Grandpa started at the noise and looked up. He struggled to his feet and Jolene was painfully aware of the fatigue on his face. Lines of concern crossed Dad's brow. Grandpa rubbed his eyes and twisted his moustache.

"Karen's just going to answer some questions for Dad," said Jolene, drawing Grandpa back onto a chair in the living room.

Dad dug a notebook out of his briefcase and motioned for Karen to be seated at the table. "Now," he began, "I think I've got everything I need up to the day of the slide. So, that morning, on April 29, 1903, when exactly did the people of Frank discover there'd been a slide?"

"Well, they heard the noise, of course," began Karen.

"It woke them?"

"Most of them were asleep, yes," agreed Karen. "A few early risers were already up in the hotels and the like." Dad jotted down some notes.

"They had to wake the guests who were leaving on the Spokane Flyer." It was Grandpa's voice and they all turned to stare at him. His eyes were closed and he was leaning back in the easy chair. Dad frowned.

"That's right," said Karen. "And, of course, there were a few who hadn't gone to bed yet."

Grandpa chuckled. "Like Diamond Bill. He'd played poker all night at the Miners' Hotel, and had just stepped outside when he heard this most unholy din and saw all these people racing about in their nightclothes. Figured he'd had too much to drink and took himself home to sleep."

Jolene laughed nervously. "He's been reading a lot," she told Dad.

Concern remained etched on Dad's forehead.

"So the story goes," Karen said, her eyes staring at the back of Grandpa's grey hair.

"So basically, then, they knew immediately there'd been a slide?" Dad continued.

"Not really," said Karen. Jolene said a silent prayer of thanks that Grandpa had decided not to answer. Maybe he'd just fall asleep. "Some thought it was an explosion in the mine, some thought it was a volcano, a hurricane even."

Grandpa snorted loudly. "And Mrs. Bailey, she even thought it was the end of the world. Climbed up on those rocks in her nightgown and started preaching that the time had come and that the righteous would be delivered, right in the midst of all that bedlam."

Jolene laughed out loud. She could just imagine Mrs.

Bailey — her nightgown flapping in the wind, her Bible in hand, and her voice raised to the heavens. Dad frowned at her and she checked her laughter.

He shuffled his papers. "So, it was only after the rocks had fallen and they discovered all the boulders that they honestly knew what had happened. Say five or ten minutes after the actual slide?"

Jolene sighed. Dad tried so hard, but he just didn't get it. The mountain face had slid, buried families, young wives, young men who had ordered wives, men gathered around a story — and Dad was interested in how many minutes it had taken.

Karen nodded, her short hair sweeping across the neckline of her blouse.

"And then they started their rescue operations?"

"Yes," said Karen. "The miners' cottages were the closest and that's the area they started looking in first."

"A white cloud was hanging over the eastern part of the town and there was a fire in the midst of it." Grandpa was talking now, talking as if nobody was there, unable to stop. "Apparently, the first group of men ran towards the blaze, but there was a big bank of mud filled with trees, logs and large stones. They could hear the screams from the slide, so they scrambled up onto the rock."

Dad fiddled with his notepad and gestured at Grandpa. "He gets like this at times," he explained to Karen. "I guess the mind goes with age." But Karen was listening.

"By the time the rescue crew arrived, they'd already pulled a man, his wife and a baby from the wreck of their house. There was another house half smashed in. They found two little girls inside, more scared than hurt and managed to get them out. One of the men found a mangled iron bed. Beside it was a young boy, dead."

"Two boys, both dead," corrected Karen.

"The parents had been crushed too, crushed in their sleep. Probably didn't even know what had happened," said Grandpa. "But outside the house, not so far away, the rescuers found an infant on top of a bale of hay. This tiny girl just lying there and not a mark on her."

Dad had stopped making notes.

"They went on searching, and all the time they were wondering what had happened to the Spokane Flyer," continued Karen. "The passenger train was late and there'd been no word of it. Of course they all knew that the main track had been completely buried and all they could do was hope that the train would stop before it ran straight into that mass of rock."

"What happened?" Jolene's voice cut into the story.

Grandpa opened his eyes. "Moments before the slide, the freight engine had been on the spur line by the mine, backing up to pick up the coal cars at the tipple. They had just hooked up when the mountain let loose. The engineer gunned it and managed to cross the wooden bridge before the rock sent it crashing into the water."

"He had two brakemen with him," said Karen, picking up where Grandpa had left off. "At first they were pretty shaken up, but then they figured that they had to do something about the incoming train. So they set out across the rocks with their lanterns to warn the engineer. It was tough going. The rocks were still hot from sliding down the mountain and it was almost impossible to see anything because of the dust cloud. One of the men couldn't keep up, but the other one groped his way around these massive chunks of rock and then finally, stumbled out onto the tracks and flashed his lantern just as the Spokane Flyer rolled through the night."

A picture of Elio flashed through Jolene's mind. His mail order bride had been on that train. At least she had been spared thanks to the brakeman.

"He was a real hero," said Karen quietly.

"The station was covered with mud, but it remained intact." Grandpa's voice again. "When the sun came up, there were limbs and carcasses everywhere — pigs, dogs, horses, people. People pinned in their beds, men naked and bleeding, women with broken bones protruding, children muddied with fear, and that poor old doctor needed everywhere and smelling of ether."

Karen rose to her feet and walked around to the picture window. "And then came the discovery that the mine entrance had been buried. All those men entombed in the mine, and a big lake forming at the entrance because the river had backed up. The rescue team roped logs together into rafts and tried to get close, but huge boulders were still tumbling down the mountainside and more than once they had to run for cover. And all the time they were thinking of those men in the mine, knowing it could have been any one of them."

"But they got out didn't they, the men in the mine?" Jolene jumped at Dad's voice. He, too, was hanging on the edge of the words.

"The rescue crew kept on, knowing they couldn't just give up, but not making much progress," said Karen. "And then late in the afternoon, a voice called from up above the mine entrance, high on the face of the mountain. It was the miners. Seems they'd known pretty quickly that something had happened. Even underground, they'd heard the roar of the slide and rock and coal had rained down on them. A rush of air had doused most of their lamps. First they'd tried to get out the main entrance, but they'd soon realized that they were trapped inside. Next, they'd explored the lower tunnel, but it was blocked and rapidly filling with water. The river had been dammed by the slide. All the airways were blocked."

"What a predicament!" said Dad.

"Those miners were sealed underground. The river was rising and not only was there no air supply, but lethal methane gas was accumulating." Karen paused. "That's when they remembered that a coal seam was visible above the mine entrance on the front face of the mountain. They decided to try and dig a raise up through the seam. It took them thirteen hours, but they succeeded," said Karen. "You should have heard the celebrating."

"I can imagine," said Dad.

Karen's nails scratched her knuckles. "The women, the wives and children, they'd been waiting all day, fearing the worst and there were their husbands, fathers, sons, brothers and uncles, tired and hungry — but alive."

Jolene could almost hear the voices shouting across the river, whooping with joy.

"Not all of them." Grandpa's voice was low and even.

Karen let out a sigh. "No, not all of them. And for some of the men in the mine who had survived, one look at the way the rocks fanned out over the area where their homes had been was pretty sobering." She shook her head. "As for the railway construction camp — the slide buried the entire crew, as well as the ranchers who lived at the base of the mountain and the men in the stable."

Jolene tried to block out the image of Robert on the pitcher's mound, Karl with Old Charlie, and the others. "What about Old Man Warner?" she whispered. "Did he make it?"

Grandpa looked up in confusion. "No, he didn't," said Karen. Dad was staring at Jolene, questions in his eyes. "He was an old trapper that lived in a tent at the base of the mountain," explained Karen.

They sat unmoving, feeling the silence surround them and, finally, quiet their thoughts.

"Well that's quite the story," said Dad after a long moment. "You two make it sound like you were there."

Jolene looked from Grandpa to Karen. Grandpa had certainly been there. Karen's eyes were distant. She scratched a mole on the back of her left hand. And suddenly Jolene remembered that gesture. It was the same one that Aunt Peggy had made in 1903. She looked at Karen closely. Her hair was grey, but her eyes were green. Could it be? Could Peggy have gone into the future and been unable to go back? She glanced at Grandpa, but he showed no sign of recognition.

"Well, I guess I'll be going if you have everything you need," said Karen, rising.

"Thank you so much for all your help. I do hope you'll come to Calgary for the opening of the exhibit." Dad stood up. "You're a terrific guide."

"And a great storyteller," added Grandpa.

Karen blushed. "As are you," she said. "You're a living history lesson."

Thoughts tumbled through Jolene's mind like boulders down the slide. A living history lesson — like Old Man Warner. She jumped to her feet. That was it. That was it! The very thing!

Chapter Fourteen

Jolene smoothed Grandpa's woolen cap and handed it to him. He set it atop his grey hair and adjusted the sleeves of his woolen jacket. It was much like the one he had left behind in Frank. "You look great," she told Grandpa.

Grandpa put an arm around her shoulders. "All this commotion over a bunch of rocks."

"Those rocks make great stories." She peered out the window of the museum through the assembling crowd. Dad was milling about, waving his arms and giving directions. And Gerard was there, too, standing next to the doors. Her heart skipped a beat.

Grandpa joined her. "Are those television people here yet?"

"All set up and ready to go. How about you?"

Grandpa shot a look at his reflection in the window. "I suppose so." He frowned playfully. "I guess I have you to thank for this."

"Hey, don't blame me. It's your own fault — you never could resist telling a good story. All I did was remind Dad of that fact. Besides," Jolene added, "it's important to tell those stories." It had taken her a long time to realize that story was such an important part of history, but it hadn't taken Dad long to figure things out once she'd told him her idea. He'd been the first to admit that he'd been enraptured listening to Grandpa and Karen, and it had been easy to convince him that the museum visitors would be, too. With his stories, Grandpa would bring history alive, add a sense of tragedy to the exhibits that Dad had so carefully constructed. At least, that's what the reporter had said yesterday after he'd met with Grandpa.

Behind them, covering one wall, was a magnificent photographic re-creation of Turtle Mountain, its face intact, before the slide. Several large boulders stood in front of the photo. On the edge of the rocks, true to its time, stood the general store on Dominion Avenue. Frank, 1903. It was in the store, just as Jolene had once found him, that Grandpa would begin his story. But as he reached the night of April 29th, the lights would go out and for ninety seconds, a deafening recording of a rock slide would fill the room. Then another superb image, this one of the slide, would be projected onto the wall, creating the effect that the mountain had slid. It had been Dad's idea and it was superb.

"Is Karen coming today?" asked Jolene.

"She is," said Grandpa.

"Will you tell her?"

Grandpa thought for a moment. "I don't know, Jo." He played with the smooth checkers on the table beside his chair.

Jolene heard the noise of the crowd outside as Michael burst through the doors. "Are you ready?" he asked them excitedly. He turned to Jolene. "But you're not even changed. Have you decided not to do it?"

Jolene grinned at him. Dad had asked her to introduce Grandpa as the town storyteller and, much to everyone's surprise, she had agreed. "I'm on my way," she said, disappearing into a side room.

A rack of clothing resembling that worn in the early 1900s hung in front of her. She slid the hangars down the rack and stopped at a pair of knee-length trousers, white shirt and cloth cap. They were the clothes she had worn in Frank. In Frank, where she had been attacked by a black bear and walked the dreadful ledge for a foul ball. In Frank, where she had survived school, helped save Peter and, she hoped, helped Daniel in his quest to be a lawyer. In Frank, where she and Grandpa had almost been buried by the slide. In Frank, where she had learned to be a risk-taker.

"You'd better hurry up," called Grandpa from the other

room. "Your dad's getting excited." She could hear Grandpa ease into his storyteller's chair.

Hangars chimed against one another and garments rustled. Jolene pulled clothes from the rack. She'd never talked in front of a big group of people like this before. She straightened her sleeves and did up her buttons. And Gerard was here; she hadn't counted on that. She slipped off her sandals and pulled on her shoes. She'd just have to imagine that they were all horses. She took a quick glance in the mirror as the exterior doors banged open and the television crew and visitors filed in.

Then she lifted the hem of her skirt and stepped out into the museum.

ABOUT THE AUTHOR

 Cathy Beveridge was born and raised in Calgary and spent four years abroad in the Middle East. While there, she developed a keen interest in writing about Canada and upon her return wrote *Shadows of Disaster*, her first time-travel adventure, which brings to life Frank Slide, Canada's deadliest rockslide. *Shadows of Disaster* has been nominated for the Rocky Mountain Book Award, the Diamond Willow Award and the Red Cedar Book Award. This was followed by her second historical adventure, *Chaos in Halifax*, where Jolene and her twin brother find themselves trapped in the devastation of the Halifax explosion. *Stormstruck*, her third book, finds Jolene shipwrecked on Lake Huron during the "Great Storm" of 1913. Her fourth book in the series, *Tragic Links*, follows the Quebec Bridge and Laurier Palace Theatre disasters. Other publications include two contemporary young-adult novels, *Offside* (Thistledown, 2001), winner of the 2003 Saskatchewan Snow Willow Award, and *One on One* (Thistledown, 2005). Some of Cathy's short stories may be found in anthologies such as *Beginnings: Stories of Canada's Past* (Ronsdale, 2001) and *Up All Night* (Thistledown, 2001). Background information for the novel is available at www.ronsdalepress.com under *Stormstruck*.